MW00478344

TRIFECTA

TIN STAR K9 SERIES - BOOK 6

JODI BURNETT

SDG PUBLISHING

Copyright © 2023 by Jodi Burnett

All rights reserved.

No part of this book may be reproduced in any form or by any electronic or mechanical means, including information storage and retrieval systems, without written permission from the author, except for the use of brief quotations in a book review.

For my Family and for Sarah and Danny – this book was written the year you got married – a truly blessed year.

TRIFECA

PROLOGUE

Barbequed ribs and baked beans had been a bad idea. Bill pressed his fist against his roiling stomach. Nerves mixed with the spicy grease gave him searing heartburn. He burped and swallowed it back as he turned the cargo van onto a shadowy, rural dirtroad deep in the southern Tennessee countryside. Spanish moss draped the trees crowding in toward them from the edge of the narrow path, lending them a haunted air. Moonlight glowed like silver icing on the lacy cover adding to the night's spooky atmosphere. Bill shuddered at the sensation, as he glanced at the man riding beside him in the passenger seat.

"We're almost there." Bill shifted to make more room for the gun he had stuffed in his pants at the small of his back.

"It's so dark out here." The second man pressed the lock on his door. "I can't see anything."

Though Bill knew the van was locked, he glanced at

his door's knob to be double certain. "This road opens up near the bridge. We'll be able to see better when we get there." The headlights pushed against the dense foliage but provided less than ten feet of visibility before the high beams died against the wall of thick vegetation.

Bill's partner for the night rubbed his hands together. "Turn up the heat. I'm freezing to death."

"That's just nerves. Quit worrying. It's all gonna go according to plan. We'll be in and out of there in less than thirty minutes. Then we'll get our reward. Ten grand is pretty good pay for a couple hours of work."

"Yeah. It is. So long as everything is copasetic."

"Stop with the fretting. You're making me nervous too." The van crept along the curvy road. "You double counted the money, right? We have the full amount?"

"Yeah, yeah. Now who's freaking out?"

Bill's shoulders were as tight as the steel cables holding up the bridge where the deal was going to go down. The structure came into view as he made the final turn toward the river. They were the first to arrive, and he coasted the van onto the wooden slats of the bridge, stopping one third of the way across. He shifted the vehicle into park but left the engine running and tapped his fingers on the steering wheel. The water in the river below flowed fast, its white ripples glittered in the night.

Five minutes later, Bill rolled down his window. Cold air fought against the heat inside the van. "I want to hear them coming," he explained. But the truth was his neck and armpits were drenched with sweat. He welcomed the brisk, damp temperature flowing in, but all he heard was the river sluicing by and a few crickets chirping weakly in the cold. In the summer the tiny critters rubbed their legs together as though their lives depended on it, but tonight their song lacked vigor.

"What's taking them so long, Bill? What do we do if they don't show?"

He wasn't sure. This was his first ever drug deal and meeting deep in the sticks—in the middle of the night— did nothing to boost his confidence. Anything could happen out here, and no one would know. The thick foliage would soak up screams and a body would be welcome food for swampy critters who devoured flesh. It would completely disappear within days. Goose bumps rippled across the surface of his arms at his dark thoughts.

Another five long minutes ticked by before a pair of truck headlights flickered through the trees on the other side of the black river. "Here they come."

The arriving vehicle's engine roared as it ascended a small hill on the way up to the bridge. Without slowing, the pickup barreled onto the bridge and came to a stop fifty feet in front of Bill's van. The truck driver flashed his headlights. Bill blinked his in return and then both vehicles slowly rolled toward the center of the bridge.

They stopped with fifteen feet to spare, and Bill waited for the newcomers to make the first move. All four truck doors opened and as many men stepped down from the cab. Bill and his partner followed suit and got out of the van, leaving their doors open in case they needed to escape in a hurry.

The truck driver nodded at them and one of his

lackeys leaned into the back door of the crew cab. He removed a cooler-sized trunk and carried it to a spot between the vehicles. The man who rode on the front passenger's side held a shotgun, giving credence to his seat position, and stood guard as the other two in their gang struggled with a large wooden crate. They dropped it on the ground next to the smaller container.

The driver yelled, "You got the money?"

"We do," Bill answered. "But I need to see the guns and check the quality of the blow, first."

"No. *First*, we see the cash," the driver barked.

Bill nodded to his partner, who leaned in and retrieved a black hard-sided suitcase. He placed it on the ground and unzipped it, opening the cover to display stacks of bundled hundred-dollar bills.

The truck driver whistled and grinned, displaying a set of crooked, tobacco-stained teeth with a missing incisor. "Okay, come on over and do your test."

Sweat trickled down Bill's back, soaking into his already damp shirt. Carrying his test kit, he approached the containers and gestured for the men to open them. Inside the wooden crate, a stack of black military-grade automatic rifles glistened up at him. His fingers itched to run along the smooth metal, but he merely nodded and turned his attention to the bricks of white powder waiting to be assessed. Bill randomly selected a bag from the second row and slit the plastic with a box cutter. He took some of the white powder from the package with the edge of his blade and weighed it on a palm-sized digital scale. The numbers blinked, and he added a touch more until he had one gram. He opened a glass vile half-filled with a clear, liquid testing-agent from his kit and poured the cocaine sample into it. When he shook the small bottle, the liquid turned dark, and his neck released a little of the tension he'd held. He breathed in, filling his lungs. "Good." He called over his shoulder. "Bring the payment."

His partner zipped the suitcase closed and carried it to the men. He set it down and reached for the crate containing the cocaine.

"Wait." The truck driver pressed the trunk back down with his boot. "You tested the coke. Now, I want to check the currency."

Bill's back muscles tightened. He wanted the transaction to be over with and to get the hell out of this swampy place. But he nodded to his cohort. Fair was fair, after all.

His partner made no move to open the suitcase. "It's all there, man. Are you planning on counting it out here?"

"Open the case." The driver's voice was low and menacing. The guard chambered a shell in his shotgun.

Sweat popped out across Bill's forehead at the familiar ratcheting sound. "Open it, you idiot. And hurry up. We all want to get out of here."

Bill's partner hesitated before he knelt and unlatched the lid. The driver pulled out several bundles of C-notes. He flipped through the bills like book pages. On the third bundle he stopped and re-flipped, pausing at the center of the stack. He plucked a few bills out of the binding, then reached for a pen he had in his front pocket. "Let's just test out a few of these Benjamins."

He smudged the felt tip across the top of the bills. Then he repeated the action a second time. Steadily, his eyes rose to meet Bill's with a heat that caused him to flinch. "This money is counterfeit. Did you assholes think we wouldn't notice?"

Bill's jaw flopped open seconds before his gaze hardened and he glared at his partner whose hand now trembled on the edge of the suitcase. "What did you do? How much did you take?" Panic rattled through Bill's voice, and he yelled, "You have to make this right!"

A shotgun blast cut off any words the kneeling man might have said in his defense. His head exploded in a shower of red mush and flecks of skull. In that second, Bill dove to his side. Terror stole his breath. He gripped the gun he'd stuffed in his waistband and fired at the man aiming the shotgun, hitting him in the chest. Bill rolled to his feet and sprinted to the van. Shielding himself behind the van door, he scrambled inside.

One of the other guards, gripping a sawed-off shotgun, charged from behind his fallen comrade. He blasted shots repeatedly at Bill. Pellets sprayed across the side of the van, propelling glass and shrapnel into his shoulder. Searing heat melted his skin and tore at the flesh underneath, the acrid scent stung his nose. Bill screamed with pain and rage. He leveled his pistol and fired at the man who wanted him dead. Bill dropped from the van to his knees in agony. With a hail Mary attempt, he raised his gun again and squeezed the trigger, sending another round into his attacker.

A responding shot burst a chunk of muscle and sinew out of Bill's thigh, misting blood across the side of the van. Bill's heart ricocheted in his chest, and he couldn't suck in any air. Pain radiated throughout his entire body. He went hot and cold all at once. His body floated light as a cotton puff until his head slammed onto the wooden planks of the bridge floor. He watched through slitted eyes as the truck's tires spun in reverse, smoke filling the wheel wells. His vision blurred and dimmed until there was nothing.

1

C olt Branson held his hand out toward his wife, Caitlyn, and pulled her to her feet. "Let's leave the old year behind us with a dance."

"And bring the new year in with a champagne kiss." Caitlyn slid her hand into his and followed him to the crowded dance floor. They were spending New Year's Eve, along with most everyone in Moose Creek, Wyoming, at The Tipsy Cow. Normally, the local bar was a dusty honky-tonk filled with ranchers and locals, but that night the owner decorated it in gold and silver—all gussied up to ring in the new year.

Colt drew his wife into his arms as they fell into the comfortable rhythm of the two-step. He glanced at the other dancers as they moved around the floor. Dylan, Caitlyn's older brother and his bride, McKenzie sashayed by. Those two got married only a couple of weeks after he and Caitlyn took their vows.

It had been an eventful summer. Too eventful. Colt's thoughts skimmed over the dark days of Caitlyn's abduction. That was the scariest time in his life, and she was still struggling emotionally with her traumatic memories of captivity. Not to mention her desperate killing of the man who attacked her. She'd stabbed him with a knife in order to save herself. Caitlyn swore she had fully recovered. She claimed she was fine, but he knew differently.

"Hey, you guys!" Caitlyn called out to her brother and new sister-in-law. She and McKenzie had been friends before Dylan came into the picture, and Caitlyn was happy that they fell in love and got married; thrilled to finally have a sister. "Have you heard from Mom and Dad?"

Dylan shook his head, but McKenzie nodded and paused their dancing. "They're celebrating New Year's Eve in Dublin."

"I'm so glad Dad agreed to go. It looks like they're both having a great time in the pictures she posts on Instagram."

Dylan chuckled, "Yeah, but now Mom's going to have to spend a week camping and fishing on the river for paybacks."

Caitlyn hit Dylan's arm with the back of her hand. "She'll have fun doing that, too. Don't underestimate her."

"I'm just relieved their cold war is no longer being staged in our house." Dylan spun McKenzie off and she waved over her shoulder.

Colt followed suit with Caitlyn. It had become miserable at the Reed ranch with Stella and John, fighting all the time. They'd entered their new stage of retired life with a crash. Both had worked hard all their lives and making the transition had been a bumpy ride. It took some serious convincing on his and Dylan's part to get John to swallow his pride and go to Ireland with Stella, but thankfully, he finally gave in.

Caitlyn gazed up at him. "I hope my parents are having a wonderful time in Dublin, but I kinda wish they were here. This is the first Christmas and New Years I've ever spent without them." Her voice was wistful, and it squeezed Colt's heart.

"But it's our first New Year's Eve as man and wife." He kissed her cheek and nuzzled her ear, making her laugh.

"You know who else isn't here... Blake and Kayla." Her dark eyes scanned the crowd.

"He's probably on call. There's always somebody who drinks too much and tries something crazy on this night of the year. I imagine the emergency room is keeping Doc hopping."

The country band's lead singer ended his song and leaned into the microphone. "The ball drops in five minutes, everyone. Make sure your glasses are full and you're ready to toast! Grab the one you love, or the one you want to love, and get ready for the countdown!" Bottles of champagne passed through the partiers who filled their glasses and waited expectantly.

"Ten, nine, eight..." The crowd shouted along with the band. "Three, two, one! Happy New Year!"

Confetti bombs popped, exploding glittering flecks of plastic and paper over the crowd. Horns blew and someone in the kitchen banged on a large pot with a wooden spoon. The sudden noise sent Caitlyn into a full-blown panic attack. Her eyes flew open wide, and she spun around, raising her arms defensively over her head before she dropped to her knees, cowering. Shocked, Colt crouched down and reached for her, but she shook him off.

"Catie! It's okay." Instantly, Colt's chest ached with remorse for bringing her. She wasn't ready. Even still— though it had been over five months. "Come here, babe." He pulled her to her feet and held her close. Her heart slammed against her chest wall so hard he could feel it through her sweater and his winter-weight flannel. "You're safe. It's okay. I've got you."

Caitlyn jerked away from him. "I'm fine." She brushed off her knees. "The noise just startled me, that's all. No need to overreact." Her voice was sharp, and she turned her back to him.

Dylan rushed to her side. "You okay, kid?"

She glared up at her brother. "I'm *fine*. I lost my balance, that's all. Why is everybody making such a big deal out of it? It's New Year's Eve. I had too much champagne. So what?" Her eyes still held remaining flecks of panic as she headed toward the exit. "I'm going to get some air." She pushed passed the men and strode out the door.

Colt grabbed her coat from her chair and ran after her. "Hey, it's too cold out here without a jacket." She stood with her back to him, her arms wrapped around her middle. He draped the coat over her shoulders. "Catie, I know you want everyone to think you're fine—that you're over the trauma of everything that happened last summer —but you're not. And that's okay. But you do need help. You need to go back to the psychologist."

"Stop telling me what I need." Her hot words puffed

white in the frozen air. "The doctor already cleared me to return to work."

"Because you told her what she wanted to hear. Listen, going back to work before you're ready isn't good for anyone. In fact, it's dangerous."

Her eyes flashed at him. "If the doctor says I'm good to go, then I am. You don't have a degree in psychology. Do you?"

"No," he slowed his breath and steadied his voice. It was getting harder to be patient with Caitlyn's stubbornness on this issue. "But I *am* the one who wakes up with you when you have nightmares, and who finds you crying in the shower." He lifted her chin and looked into her eyes. "Would it hurt to talk with another doctor?"

"I didn't hide anything from my psychologist, Colt. What happened to me really sucked, and sometimes I still have dreams about it, you're right, but I need to move on. I'm beginning to think you just want me to stay home now that we're married."

"Come on, Catie. That's not fair, and you know that isn't true." But inside, he wondered if she might be right. He would never stand in the way of her career, but he'd be lying to himself if he didn't admit he'd like to keep her close, to keep an eye on her and protect her. After all, her abduction shook him deeply, too.

"I think it *is* true. You'd just love it if I stayed home and had babies." She stomped off toward their car.

Colt ran his hand down the back of his neck and watched her go. *Babies?* They hadn't even discussed starting their own family. Not really. Not since they discovered he already had a son he'd known nothing

13

about. They'd been working on coming together as a family with Jace and dealing with Allison, the boy's mother, and all the hoops they had to go through to make that situation work.

"Catie, wait!" he called and ran after her.

At their cabin home, Caitlyn was quiet as she changed her clothes for bed. He held her in the darkness while they slept. At 6:00 a.m. her phone rang and woke him. Caitlyn grumbled and buried her head under her pillow, so Colt reached for the device. Dirk Sterling, his wife's mentor and sometimes partner's face lit up the screen, and Colt answered.

"Hey, Dirk. Caitlyn's sleeping. Can I give her a message?"

"Too much partying last night, huh?" Dirk chuckled. "Tell her to get her ass out of bed. We've finally gathered the hard evidence we need to arrest Anthony Trova. NYPD has clear video surveillance of him present at a drug deal. Combined with Tito Garza's testimony we finally have the green light to bring him in. I figured Caitlyn would want to be in on the bust."

"I don't know, Dirk." Colt rolled over and hung his legs over the edge of the bed. "Can you hold on a sec?" He grabbed a sweatshirt and left the room, softly closing the door behind him. "I'm not sure she's ready to come back to work yet."

"I thought the therapist cleared her. Isn't she already back at work?"

"Officially, she is, but mostly she's been doing computer searches at the Casper office or from home, following paper trails." Switching the phone to his other hand, Colt pulled on his shirt and trudged into the kitchen to make a pot of coffee. "She's been giving everybody the tough-guy act, but I'm not buying it."

"I know you're probably worried about her, but she has to get back on the horse sometime."

"You're right, but I'm not sure now's the time." Colt chuffed, "Maybe she could just get on a pony."

Dirk was quiet for a few seconds before he said, "The thing is, she needs a solid win to get her confidence back. And now that I think about it, I might know just the pony-ride that could give it to her while easing her back to the job."

"Personally, I think some more time off would be better. I'm hoping to get her to see another doctor, for a second opinion. She's still having nightmares, and last night she had an episode when the party poppers went off at midnight. I was hoping she might like to stay home a little longer and help Dylan and McKenzie finish setting up their dog breeding and training facility."

Dirk laughed. "You know her better than that. Sounds like you're being a bit overprotective, Sheriff. Knowing Caitlyn, work will be the most healing thing she can do. Listen, I've got to go, but I'll look into that job I'm thinking about. It's a simple property seizure. What could happen?"

2

I t was around 11:00 a.m. when Renegade, licked
Caitlyn's cheek. Without opening her eyes, she
swatted at him. He swiped his warm, wet tongue
across her nose. Finally, she rolled out of bed. "Renegade!"
she grumbled as she wiped her face on the soft sleeve of
her flannel sleep shirt. Her head pounded, which didn't
make sense. She'd only had two or three beers and a glass
of champagne over the course of the whole night. She'd
been tipsy, maybe, but nothing that warranted the bongo
drums thumping inside her skull. On the way to the
kitchen searching for a desperately needed cup of coffee,
she stopped in the bathroom and swallowed a couple of
extra strength Tylenol capsules.

Colt wasn't in the living room or kitchen when she
trudged out, but he'd left a note on the counter. He
explained he'd gone into the office for the morning to
help process the few drunks his deputy, Wes, had brought
in last night, and that he'd be back around three. Caitlyn
glanced at the stove clock and decided she had plenty of

time to drive out to her family's ranch and check out the progress Dylan and McKenzie had made on their new K9 breeding and training facility.

"You want to go see Larry, Ember, Athena and her pups?" Caitlyn asked Renegade, referring to Dylan and McKenzie's dog family. Her own Belgian Malinois barked, sending a sharp dagger of sound into Caitlyn's brain. He sat, sweeping his tail across the rough-hewn floor.

After nursing her coffee and getting dressed, Caitlyn drove with Renegade to the other side of Moose Creek, out to the family ranch where she'd grown up. She slowed as she passed her parents' rambling log cabin home and the big red barn and followed the fresh cut road that led to the dog kennels. She was impressed with the training facility Dylan had built for his new wife and business partner. McKenzie was in the yard working with some of Athena's puppies who were now almost six months old. Her friend waved as Caitlyn parked and let Renegade out of her new, specially outfitted, US Marshal K9 Explorer.

"Hey, Kenze! Looks like things are going gangbusters around here," Caitlyn called as she approached the fence with her dog. Two adorable Malinois puppies gamboled over to them, yapping, and wagging their tails.

"I know! Can you believe how much Dylan has gotten done? Wait 'til you see the inside."

Renegade sniffed at the small dogs through the chain link, and Caitlyn reached over the gate to pet their cute fuzzy heads. "How's the puppy training coming along?"

"They're ready. They all have basic obedience and have started on scent tracking. I'm hoping that some of the new buyers will want to put more training on them and will hire me to do it. But usually, most K9 handlers like to add the finishing touches to their own dogs."

"Are they all sold, then?"

"Yep! With Tony's recommendation down in Florida, the pups that weren't previously claimed are headed south. I'm shipping these final two out next week. One to Philadelphia and the other to Boise."

"What will you do with yourself without a brood of puppies to train?" Caitlyn teased.

"Prepare to breed and have more." McKenzie reached over the fence and patted Renegade on the head. "You ready to be the first sire of Reed Ranch K9s?"

Renegade licked her hand, raising his paw and batting at the air. McKenzie took hold of the paw he offered. "Good boy, Ren." She ruffled his fur once more. "Let me put the puppies in their pen, and I'll meet you inside in the office. Dylan's in there somewhere."

Caitlyn nodded and headed toward the new building. Inside, the kennel was warm and bright, naturally lit by skylights and windows. Her brother had spared no effort in building the perfect space for McKenzie and her training business. Caitlyn found Dylan in a storage room at the back of the business office organizing bags of food, toys of all types, basic K9 first aid supplies, and training equipment.

"You've done a tremendous job on this place, Dyl."

Her brother looked up and grinned. "Thanks. There's plenty of room for you if you decide you'd like to help Kenze out in the business."

Caitlyn drew back. "Uh… thanks? But I have a job, remember?"

"Well, yeah, but Colt mentioned you might be taking some more time off."

"Did he?" Irritation smoldered underneath her skin. Colt had no business talking about her behind her back to Dylan. Her husband needed to accept the fact that she was going to go back in the field and deal with it.

"Don't get all pissed off at Colt. He's just looking out for you."

"Yeah, well, I don't need him to do that. I'm driving down to Casper on Monday and hopefully I'll get a field assignment soon. It's been too long as it is."

Dylan wiped his hands on a rag and stepped out of the backroom into the light of the office. "Are you sure you're ready? There's no rush, you know."

"It's been half a year since I've seen any action. I'm beyond ready. Regardless of what my over-protective husband says."

Dylan shrugged. "Come here." He strode past her out of the office. "I want to show you the bathing station I just completed."

"Plush!" A large elevated stainless-steel dog bath stood under a coiled shower hose. He had bracketed dog shampoo and conditioner pump bottles to the wall next to a long tube that looked like the vacuum at the carwash. "What's this?"

"That's the hair dryer, or *fur* dryer in this case." Dylan flipped the machine on, and a strong flow of warm air blew out. Renegade barked at the noisy hose.

Caitlyn snatched the nozzle and aimed the airflow at her brother. "This place is amazing. It's like a spa. The dogs Kenzie trains will never want to leave." Dylan clicked off the motor, and Caitlyn followed him past a table filled with grooming tools. Her phone buzzed and she answered. "This is Reed."

"Are you keeping the name Reed? Or will you be changing it to Branson?" Caitlyn's boss, US Marshal of the Wyoming region, Leila Williams's voice echoed through the speaker.

"I'm using Reed professionally, ma'am. What can I do for you?"

"I wanted to catch you before you headed to Casper. There's a prisoner transfer I'd like you to handle on the way to a longer assignment outside the town of Shelbyville, Tennessee."

"Yes, ma'am. What's going on in Tennessee?"

"US Marshals down there recently seized a racehorse property from the owner who is drowning in gambling debt and owes hundreds of thousands of dollars in back taxes. Apparently, he entered the drug and gun smuggling world to pay off his liability. Only, when his most recent deal went south, he fled the country to escape the dealer he pissed off. We believe he's hiding out in Puerto Rico, and a contingent of Marshals from the Tennessee office lit out after him. Which leaves their department with a high-dollar racehorse farm that needs watching over until they can catalog all the assets and auction them off.

"Deputy Sterling suggested that you'd be the perfect candidate to assist in this job, since you have horse experience and all. So, I offered to send you down there to help."

Caitlyn stopped in the center of the aisle, perching her free hand on her hip. Her brows drew together. "So, basically I'd be horse sitting?" She did her best to temper the indignation out of her tone.

"There's more to it than that. A team is already in place going through the house creating an inventory of all the personal items. Eventually, they'll set up an auction to sell off the property, the household items, and the horses. For the time being, they need someone capable and trustworthy to care for the horses and guard the property at night. You'll be staying at the farm until they sell everything."

"If the owner skipped the country, who will I be guarding the property from?"

"It probably won't amount to anything, but the owner left a pissed-off loan shark and an even more livid drug and gun runner in the lurch. I'm sure they're more interested in going after the man who left them hanging, than his ranch, but we need to be vigilant. We also have a single witness in custody who was in on the deal. He's currently in the hospital recovering from a gunshot wound, but as soon as he testifies, we'll enter him into WITSEC. Honestly, I think this is the perfect assignment for you and Renegade to dip your toes back in the water."

Caitlyn pushed aside the sense that she was being coddled and patted on her head. She was a competent Deputy Marshal who was now tasked with feeding horses and making lists of household items. But, if this was the row she had to hoe to get back to work, she'd do it. She suppressed a frustrated sigh. "When do I need to be there?"

"I'd like you to leave today, if possible. You can take care of the prison transfer on your way to Tennessee. I need you to stop by Cañon City, Colorado, to pick up a female inmate who needs transferring to the Arkansas Department of Corrections. The facility is just across the Mississippi river from Memphis. The transfer will take two days. You'll have one stop over in Oklahoma City. US Marshals there will assist you for the night. The next day you'll drive to New Port, Arkansas to drop off the prisoner, then continue to the horse estate in Tennessee the following morning."

"Got it. I'll organize things on my end. If I head out for Cañon City around 4:00 a.m. tomorrow, that'll put me at the prison around eleven."

"Perfect. I'll have my admin send you all the details and paperwork. I'd like to know when you arrive in Tennessee."

"Yes, ma'am." As soon as Caitlyn was off the phone, she googled Shelbyville, Tennessee and checked the weather. *At least it'll be warmer down there.*

Dylan interrupted her focus. "Who was that? Sounded like work. You're going to Cañon City?"

Caitlyn looked up at her brother and pulled her mind from her job back to the kennel. "Yes. Then, Tennessee. I have to leave super early in the morning, so I better head back home to pack."

"What's the job?" Dylan tugged on his trim beard, concern filling his dark eyes. "I mean… are you ready?"

She narrowed her eyes at him. "I've *been* ready. Finally, I have a chance to prove it—sort of. A couple of admins could handle this easy job, but if it's what I have to do to earn my spot back, then it's what I'll do." She explained what she knew about the assignment.

After saying her goodbyes, Caitlyn and Renegade left for home. She called Colt on the road. "Hey, my boss called me in to do a prison transfer and then I'm headed to Tennessee to babysit some hoity-toity horse property. Nothing very exciting, but at least I'll get away from the office work they've stuck me with lately."

"When do you have to leave?" Colt sounded distracted. She'd expected him to resist her going back to the job.

"At four in the morning."

"When? Sorry, I was reading something. Did you say four? That's awfully sudden."

She laughed, hoping to keep things light. "Crime doesn't wait for business hours. Actually, I'm just doing an easy prisoner transfer and then helping inventory a seized horse property in Tennessee. I don't think I'll be gone too long."

"I wish you didn't have to leave right away. I just got off the phone with my attorney. He sent over another packet of information regarding the remaining hoops I still need to jump through to gain 50/50 parenting rights for Jace."

"Well, good. You can focus on that while I'm gone."

"It involves you too, you know." An edge crept into Colt's voice. "Are you sure about this, Catie? Are you really up for going back into the field? What about last night? Your reaction to—"

"This is an easy, no stress, no danger job, Colt," Caitlyn interrupted. "I have no doubt I can handle it. And the best part is I'll be able to prove to you, and Dirk apparently, that I am completely *fine*."

"Dirk?"

"Yes, he's the one who butted in and suggested to Marshal Williams that she assign me to this boring duty. I'd so much rather be going to New York with him." Colt sighed but said nothing, so Caitlyn changed the subject. "What all do you still have to do to get 50/50 parenting time?"

"I have to continue with reunification therapy with Jace, but since we've been successful with our days together and the occasional overnights, we can begin working toward having him stay with us every other weekend."

"I'll do whatever you need me to do to help, as soon as I get back."

"Thanks, but I wish you didn't have to leave so early. Jace will be at our house tomorrow for the day, and I was hoping we could do something together, all three of us. By the way, we need to make a decision about which house we're going to live in and get busy with building on a second bedroom."

Caitlyn bit down on her lower lip to keep her irritation to herself. They'd been over this. She didn't want to give up her cabin and property, but Colt was adamant about being closer to Jace's mom and the school. "Well, you know how I feel. Besides, growing up on a ranch with plenty of room to play was a good way to grow up for me and my brothers. We weren't close to the school, and we did just fine."

"Yeah, but your parents lived together and didn't have to divide their time with you."

She swallowed a retort about none of this being her

fault and asked, "What are your plans with Jace tomorrow?"

"I'm going to take him golfing."

"Golfing? In January? Not to mention, you don't golf!" Caitlyn turned onto the gravel road leading to her cabin. Renegade sat up, ready to jump out of the Explorer for a potty break and to check the property perimeter. "What are you thinking?"

Colt chuckled. "I thought it could be something we learn together, so I booked a class with the pro at the golf club. They have an indoor simulator we can start practicing on. Allison's husband was a golfer, and he'd promised to teach Jace, but never got a chance before he was killed."

Caitlyn pulled up to her beloved cabin. She turned off the engine and sat back to look at her property. She'd bought this place all on her own and had made a life there. She glanced over to her side yard where the K9 training obstacle course that Logan built for her was now covered in snow. Renegade and she had spent hours out there practicing. They created several running paths through the surrounding woods, and she'd even planted some aspen trees to shade the front porch. This place was hers and she was proud of it.

"Come on Ren," she sighed. "We need to get packed up and make something for dinner. We've got an early morning tomorrow."

3

Colt got up at 3:30 a.m. with Caitlyn and made sure her car started in the freezing middle-of-the-night temperature. While she was in the shower, he poured the first pot of coffee into a thermos for her to take on her long drive. Then he made a second pot. Now that he was up, he'd never get back to sleep.

On her way out the door, Colt pulled his wife into his arms. "I wish I knew how long you're going to be gone. I hate this open-ended stuff."

"It shouldn't be long. It's just a matter of feeding horses and waiting for the property auction to take place." She pressed up on her toes and kissed him. "I'll call you tonight from Oklahoma. Stay warm!" She kissed him again and then pulling the hood on her coat over her head, she called to Renegade, and they dashed out to her Explorer.

From the front picture window, Colt watched her drive away until he could no longer see her taillights, then he padded into the kitchen to pour himself a huge mug of coffee. He lit a fire and settled in to wait for the sun to rise.

At 9:30 a.m. sharp, Colt rapped on the Snows' front door. His breath puffed in white plumes while he waited. Several minutes later, he knocked again. Voices sounded from behind the door before Allison pulled it open and peered out. Her blonde hair curled in a perfect frame around her face, and she'd obviously taken great care with her make-up, which seemed odd to Colt so early on a blustery winter Saturday.

"Hey," Colt shoved his cold hands into his jacket pockets and breathed in the homey smells of baking that wafted out the door. "Is Jace ready to go?"

"Where exactly are you taking him?" Allison's artfully drawn brows rose over hard blue eyes.

"First, breakfast, then up to the golf club." He peered into the living room behind her looking for his son. Allison's father sat in a recliner by a cheerful fire, eating a muffin and staring intently at his iPad.

"He's already eaten breakfast." Challenge settled on Allison's expression.

Colt resisted rising to the bait. "I'll have him home at seven tonight."

"My mother serves dinner at five."

"I'll feed him dinner."

"Colt, Jace needs consistency. You can't just force him into *your* schedule. You need to accommodate *his*."

"Can we not start this again?" Colt wished Jace would come to the door. Allison was more civil in his presence. "I *am* accommodating his schedule. That's why he'll have dinner before I bring him back."

"Hmf," Allison snorted. "You know, if I had my own house, I could ease up on these things, but as guests in my parents' home, I have no say."

Myrna, Allison's mother appeared behind her, a faded version of her pretty daughter. "Don't be silly, Allison, we are happy to work around you and Jace. You know that." She smiled up at him. "Good morning, Colt. Jace is getting his coat. He's excited to see you."

"Mother, stay out of this," Allison snapped.

Colt bobbed his chin at Myrna. "Thank you, Mrs. Snow."

Jace squeezed by his mother to get out the door while zipping his jacket. "Hi Colt! Ready?"

Allison sighed. "You could say, 'excuse me,' and tell me goodbye."

Halfway to Colt's Jeep, the boy turned. "Bye, Mom. Come on, Colt!"

Allison reached out and clutched Colt's arm. "Jace and I truly need to find our own place if we're going to stay in Moose Creek, and I can't afford that on my own."

"I know. I've been trying to find a solution. Please, try to be patient."

"When will I be getting your back child support money? That would help."

"As soon as the judge determines the amount. I'll have to make payments. I don't have enough cash to pay it in full."

"I'd prefer a lump sum. I could use it for a down payment on a house."

Heat climbed Colt's neck and his jaw muscles flexed, but he kept his voice level. "I'll do the best I can." He knew it would be better for Jace and Allison to have their own place, but the only way he could see that happening was if he and Caitlyn let them move into whichever one of their houses they decided not to keep. He couldn't see Caitlyn easily agreeing to give up the cabin and have Jace and Allison move in there. He understood his wife wouldn't be happy with that idea, but as Sheriff, it would be better for him to live closer to town. He let out a puff of frustration mulling over the situation on the way to his Jeep. *Allison probably wouldn't want to live in the country, anyway.* He supposed he could move them into his house in Moose Creek, but Caitlyn wouldn't react well to the idea of him housing Allison there either. There was no easy answer.

After stopping by the cafe, where Jace put down enough buttery pancakes to make Colt wonder if Allison had told the truth about their son already eating breakfast, they drove up the winding road to the golf course. Snow fell in hard BB-sized pellets against the windshield, and Colt bumped up the heat.

"Have you ever been golfing before?" Colt asked as he pulled into a spot in the club's mostly empty parking lot.

Jace cocked his chin sideways in thought. "Not really. My dad let me hit some plastic balls in our front yard, but his clubs were too long. He said he'd get me my own, but..." The boy dropped his chin to his chest.

A lump formed in Colt's throat, and he gripped Jace's narrow shoulder. "I know you miss him. I'm sorry you didn't have the chance to learn golf with him, but I hoped you'd like to take some lessons with me. You probably already know more about golf than I do."

"How can we learn inside? Is there a putt-putt course, or something?" Jace jumped out of the car and ran toward the door. Colt hurried to catch up.

A man dressed in gray wool slacks and a light-blue golf sweater greeted them as they entered the pro shop. "Hi Sheriff." He shook Colt's hand. "And this must be your son."

Jace glanced up at the man but then darted to a row of golf clubs. He pulled one out of its stand and held it in both hands, swinging it at an imaginary ball.

"Jace, be polite. Come back and say hello," Colt crooked his finger at his son.

Jace sighed and dropped the club back into its slot. He returned to the grown-ups and peered up. "Hi."

"Shake the man's hand." Colt rested his hand on Jace's shoulder.

A skeptical look filled the boy's eyes. "I thought only old guys did that."

Colt grinned in spite of himself. "Old guys learned their manners when they were young. Just like you." He nudged the boy's arm, and Jace held out his hand.

"Nice to meet you. I'm Dan—"

"Mr. Naughton, to you Jace," Colt interrupted.

"I'm the golf pro here at the club, and I'll be your coach today. Let's go in the back where the course simulator is and get you fitted to the right size of practice clubs."

For the next two hours father and son learned about the different golf clubs, how to grip them, and the basics of a golf swing. As they put away their equipment, Colt asked, "Did you have a good time?" Jace smiled up at him and bobbed his head. "You were really getting the hang of putting. I can't wait till spring when the course opens up and we can practice for real."

"Yeah, but can we come here again before then? This was awesome!" Jace bounced on his toes before he ran out to the pro shop. Colt finished putting away his clubs and followed. He came around the corner in time to see his son run headlong into a dark-haired man standing at the counter.

"Whoa, little man." Blake Kennedy, the town's general practitioner, bent and held out his hands to keep Jace from stumbling. He glanced up at Colt with his bright blue eyes and then smiled down at the boy. "You must be Jace. I've heard a lot about you from Caitlyn." Blake stood and held his hand out to Colt. "Sheriff."

"Doc." The men shook hands, before Blake's gaze shifted beyond Colt. "Catie's not here," Colt answered Blake's unasked question. "She's on her way to Tennessee. What are you doing here in the dead of winter?"

"Ordering new clubs for next season." Blake handed a credit card to the clerk. "How are you? Looks like you're enjoying some time with your son."

"We're good. Trying to learn this crazy game together." Colt rested his hand on Jace's sandy blond head. "You?"

"Hanging in there." Blake lowered his voice. "Kayla and I recently ended things. She's back in Arizona now. How is Caitlyn?"

A wariness tightened Colt's chest. "She's doing alright. She left town this morning. I'm sorry to hear about Kayla. I thought you two were..."

"Yes, I had hoped so, but..." Blake glanced down before

returning his penetrating gaze back to Colt. "So, Caitlyn is back at work?"

"Yeah, but I have to admit I'm worried about her. I'm not sure she's emotionally ready to return to her job yet. Her abduction last summer really did a number on her. But you know Catie. She's impossible to hold back."

"Did she pass her psych eval? I thought she was still in therapy."

Colt wasn't sure how much to share. Blake was Caitlyn's doctor, but there was more to it than that. The two of them had dated a couple of times before Colt and Caitlyn got back together, and their continued friendship often made Colt uncomfortable. Sometimes he felt like Blake was still interested in Caitlyn. The situation was murky. "Catie passed her evaluation, but she also knows what the doctors want to hear. Her therapist gave her the thumbs up, but…"

"But you're worried?"

"It's just that she's still having nightmares."

"Anything else concerning you?"

Colt glanced around the shop to buy time. He noticed a kid's section with books and trinkets. "Jace, why don't you check out those books. See if there's one you'd like." Jace zipped off away from the adults. "She had a reaction to the sound of the poppers on New Year's Eve. I think she's still struggling with some PTSD from last summer."

Blake nodded. "That's to be expected. What we want is to see her continually improving. It could take years before she's truly past the trauma."

"Sure, but how do we know if she's ready to go back to work? To carry a firearm? To face the stress of her job?"

"For now, we trust Caitlyn's therapist. I've met her. She has years of experience doing this type of work." Blake took back his charge card and slid it into his wallet. "But I'd like to see Caitlyn for a checkup when she gets home. When do you expect her?"

4

US Deputy Marshal, Dirk Sterling, sat on the corner of a table in the briefing room on the 8th Floor at 137 Centre Street, in New York City—the offices of New York Police Department's Organized Crime Control Bureau. Others in the room represented the US Marshals Service, the FBI and NYPD. All were members of the joint task force assembled to bring in Anthony Trova, mob boss of the Trova Crime Syndicate. For Dirk, this case was a pinnacle in his career. Trova was at the root of several drug crimes and murders in Montana and Wyoming that Dirk had been investigating for a more than a year.

He was desperate to bring Trova in because the man was a murdering son-of-a-bitch and the ultimate cause of his partner, Sam Dillinger's death. Dirk only wished his good friend and sometimes partner, Caitlyn Reed, could be here with him to bring the dirt bag to justice. But this wasn't the type of job someone still recovering from trauma should be involved in. She needed a gentle re-entry into work. And this was not it. Trova wasn't one who'd come in without a fight.

Special Agent Isaacson of the FBI took the lead on the investigation. Technically, Dirk outranked the guy, but he didn't care. Dirk's only concern was taking the mob boss down—not who got credit for the arrest.

Isaacson called for the individual investigation reports. The FBI team reported that Trova's wife and family were in residence in their mansion compound out on Long Island, but the team had not spotted Anthony Trova himself.

"Sterling." Isaacson's piercing eyes turned toward him. "You've been staking out Trova's Manhattan apartment. What's your report?"

Dirk ran a hand down the leg of his black jeans and cleared his throat. "The only movement at that location was when his wife and daughter left the apartment three days ago. One of our cars followed them out to the Long Island residence, where they've been since. No other movement at the apartment."

"So, he never showed up at either location, not even for the holidays?" Isaacson flipped through a typed report.

"No." Dirk pressed his shoulders back against the dissatisfaction weighing down on them. He'd wanted to make the move on Trova when they last saw him, two days before Christmas, but the 'powers that be' decided to wait. Now, the mob boss was in the wind. Again. If Trova suspected they were on to him, they might never find him. Certainly not in the US, anyway.

When all the teams reported the same inability to locate the syndicate leader, the conversation moved onto their next steps. At the end of the meeting, Dirk nodded to Hank Flannigan, the rookie deputy marshal assigned to him. "Let's go lean on my CI."

Dirk and Hank drove their rental car to a restaurant in Little Italy. A host showed them to a red-and-white checked table and brought them a basket of fresh bread. When their waiter delivered Dirk's Alfredo sauce-laden pasta, he asked, "Is Vic Castellano in the back?" The server nodded. "Will you ask him to come out?"

"Of course, sir. But if anything is wrong, I'll be happy to make it right." The young man's dark eyes scanned the table searching for his error.

"Don't worry, nothing's wrong. Your manager is an old friend of mine. That's all." Looking relieved, the waiter hurried to the kitchen. Minutes later, a slight man with slicked-back black hair, wearing a suit cut from shiny blue fabric, made his way across the dining room.

Castellano's coffee-colored eyes darted around the restaurant, and he slid his hands into his trouser pockets. "Sterling. What are you doing in the Big Apple?"

Dirk swallowed a mouthful of the creamy, garlic fettuccini. "I'm looking for information regarding Anthony Trova. Any word on the street?"

The manager rolled his shoulders. He glanced at the dining room behind him and lowered his voice. "That's a dangerous name to be bouncing around. Besides, why would *I* know anything about him?"

Dirk leaned back in his chair. "Do you?"

"Nothin' that means anything." Castellano crossed and uncrossed his arms, finally settling on stuffing his hands into his pants pockets. "Nothin' that'd help you."

"How do you know?" Dirk studied the informant as the man shifted his weight back and forth. "I'm looking for one of his associates. Someone Trova spends time with. I just need a name."

Castellano shrugged. A bell rang and the door to the restaurant opened. His eyes flew to the new customers huddled at the entrance. He tossed his chin at the host who rushed to greet them. "I don't know. Last time he was here he had a chick called Lulu on his arm. I seen her with him a bunch. That's all I know."

"Lulu? Do you have a last name or an address?"

"An address? Yeah, right. I think her last name is Gartrell or something like that. But it's not like we're friendly acquaintances, you know?"

"Yeah, okay. What does this woman look like?"

Castellano pulled his hands from his pockets, and he rotated his diamond pinky ring with his thumb. "I don't know, man. Blonde, but fake. Platinum, like Marilyn Monroe."

"You just described half of Midtown."

"Nah, man. She's gorgeous. I heard he keeps her in a place over in Brooklyn. Park Slope, I think. Yeah."

"Good work, Vic. You're doing well here. Keep it up."

"I'm trying man, but it doesn't help to have the Feds poking around."

"Well, keep your eyes and ears open. Call me if you learn anything about where Trova is these days. Got it?"

"Yeah, yeah. I gotta go." Castellano stopped at several tables to greet guests on his way back to his office.

Hank stabbed a cheese covered ravioli with his fork.

"Lulu Gartrell in Park Slope. Shouldn't be too hard to find," he scoffed.

"Maybe. Her apartment is probably owned by some fake company. We'll go over there and look around after lunch." Dirk swirled a heap of fettuccini onto his fork and his stomach rumbled in anticipation. It was fortunate that his CI worked at a restaurant that served such good food. The partners finished up their meal and declined dessert, though Castellano's restaurant was famous for their cannoli. They had work to do.

Sleepy behind the wheel after his rich meal, Dirk drove across Brooklyn Bridge while Hank searched on his phone for Lulu Gartrell. He found the woman listed on Google as a local singer.

"Check it out, boss. Lulu has a gig tonight at a club in Park Slope."

"Doesn't get easier than that. Put the address in the GPS." Dirk drove through the streets around the club to familiarize himself with the area. Once they were comfortable with the geography, they spent the next couple of hours wandering through the indoor displays at the Prospect Park Zoo, killing time before they went to see Lulu perform at the neighborhood bar.

The pub was smaller than Dirk expected, but he and Hank blended in well enough with the crowd. As well as men from Montana could fit in with trendy Brooklynites, anyway. They both ordered Cokes and found a place to stand against a counter mounted on an interior brick wall at the back of the room. It was another half hour before a band took the small stage.

Dirk had no doubt that the singer was Lulu Gartrell. She was exactly how Vic described her—curvy, with white-blond hair, and rocking the bombshell style from last century. Dirk waited, enjoying the show, until the first break. When the band filed off the stage, he followed the musicians behind a faded blue-velvet curtain, leaving Hank to keep watch from the front. Dirk entered a hallway with three doors. Two led to restrooms, and the third door opened to a greenroom of sorts. He leaned against the open doorway and watched as the band members poured their drinks and sat. The lead guitarist noticed him and asked what he wanted.

"Lulu Gartrell?"

The beauty turned sparkling eyes toward him. "Yeah, that's me. Who are you?"

"Mind if I speak to you in the hallway for a minute?"

"I guess." She glanced around at her friends, but when none of them objected, she followed Dirk out of the room. "What's up? Do I know you?"

"I'm a business colleague of Tony Trova's. I was told you know him?"

Lulu's eyes lost their shine and narrowed. "Yeah, I know that bastard."

Dirk's brows shot up. "I thought you two..."

"That was then, this is now. He's a total asshole, and if you're a friend of his, *you* probably are too." Lulu turned back toward the breakroom, but Dirk caught ahold of her arm.

"Wait. I'm *not* a friend of his. In fact, I'm inclined to agree with your opinion of him. He owes me money. Any idea where I can find him?"

"How should I know? Last I heard he took off with that slime-ball, Eddie Fusco, in some ridiculous RV."

"An RV? Where were they going?"

"Who knows? My gawd, those idiots could be anywhere. They're always going on about driving down south on some pathetic midlife crisis road trip. How stupid is that when they could just fly there on Tony's jet?"

"You sound upset. Is that because he didn't ask you to go?"

"Lord no. What would I want to drive all the way down to the gawd-forsaken Everglades for? I have a gig." She gestured to the curtain and the stage beyond. "I'm just pissed because Tony refused to wait just one extra day so he could see me sing." Lulu stuck out her glossy, pink lower lip.

"He left yesterday?"

"Yeah, him and Eddie, and Eddie's stupid dog. That mutt's more important than me!"

Dirk nodded sympathetically. "What's his RV like? Did you see it?"

Lulu's eyes narrowed again. "Why're you askin' about the RV?"

He had pushed that topic too far. "Just wondering. I'm trying to imagine driving an RV through Brooklyn. That must have been a sight." He chuckled.

"Right? I imagine they skirted the city on the Beltway and crossed over to Jersey. They're probably in Virginia by now. They're so lame!"

"No kidding. Well, if you hear from him, tell him his friend Marshal was looking for him, will ya?"

"Sure, Marshal." Lulu pressed her small hand against

his chest and plucked at a button on his shirt with bright pink nails that matched her full lips. "Are you staying for the show? You could maybe buy me a drink, after?"

Dirk took her hand and kissed her fingertips. "Nothin' I'd like more, but I can't tonight. Raincheck?"

"Anytime," she cooed. "Unless Tony's in town, of course." She winked at him and turned back to the break-room. Dirk watched her luscious hips sway as she walked away. It had been far too long since he'd enjoyed the company of a woman. Other than Caitlyn anyway, but even though his partner was a beauty, she was a wildcat. Not one to be tamed. Besides, she was happily married to a man Dirk admired, so he stopped his thoughts there. Dirk strode out to the bar and gestured for his partner to meet him outside.

"According to Lulu, Trova's on his way down south in an RV. He and a friend left yesterday. Call the Virginia and North Carolina State Patrols and have them on the lookout. Check to see if there's any record of Trova or a guy named Eddie Fusco recently purchasing or regis-tering an RV in New York."

"They're in an RV? Any description?"

"Yeah, an RV with two aging criminals and a dog." It wasn't much, but it was all they had. Presumably, Trova was no longer in New York, which was both good and bad. They'd have to hunt him down again, but he wasn't in his own stomping grounds where he could easily hide.

5

Caitlyn held open the door for the single seat in her Explorer available for prisoners. Because of Renegade's in-car kennel, the space left for suspects and criminals was small and uncomfortable. The woman, Maisy Conn, whom Caitlyn was transporting to Arkansas, glared at her as she descended the steps from the prison gate.

"You expect me to ride in that tiny space the whole way?"

"Better than walking," Caitlyn responded as she guided the woman inside, covering her head so she wouldn't bump it going in.

Maisy sat, and Caitlyn secured the woman's seatbelt. Renegade peered through the slats separating him from the prisoner and emitted a threatening guttural-rumble from his throat.

"Oh, hell no! I ain't riding in a car next to some rabid beast growling at me the whole way."

Caitlyn shut the car door and went around to slide in

behind the steering wheel. "He won't growl at you the *whole* way. Not if you sit there and behave, anyway." She started the engine, waved at the guards as she left the prison grounds, and drove along the barren road leading away from the Cañon City penitentiary. "We have a long day of driving ahead, so I suggest you settle in."

They hadn't made it to I-25 before Maisy started sneezing. Caitlyn watched her in the rearview mirror as Maisy's eyes and nose ran like a stream. "You've got to be kidding me. Are you allergic to dogs?"

"You think?" Maisy wiped her face on her sleeve. "You've gotta get me out of here."

"No can do, but I'll stop and get you some Benadryl or something on the way. Is this allergy listed in your prison record?"

"Why would it be? There ain't any dogs in the slammer." Maisy sneezed, broadcasting a mucus spray across the plexiglass barrier between her and the front seat. "I need some allergy medicine right now, before I stop breathing."

Caitlyn's lip curled in disgust. She spotted a gas station ahead and pulled up to the convenience store. "I'll be right back. Renegade will keep an eye on you."

"Whatever, bitch. Just get me my medicine." Maisy sneezed and rubbed her eyes, jangling the chain connecting her cuffs.

Inside, Caitlyn found a small packet of Benadryl and snagged a bottle of Dr. Pepper while she was at it. As she paid for her items, she noticed two men near her car. One of them reached for Maisy's doorhandle and tried to open it. Fortunately, it was locked, but the action was enough for Caitlyn to toss a bill on the counter and run outside.

"Hey! US Marshals! Get away from the car!" she commanded. Inside the Explorer, Renegade barked furiously, like he wanted to tear the men to shreds.

The taller of them turned to face her. He made a slinky movement, swinging his arms in a gesture that resembled a shrug, and laughed. "We're just looking at your puppy. No problems here, officer." One of his hands dipped behind his back and flew out again, holding a gun which he pointed at Caitlyn. "I'm just gonna need you to unlock the car door."

Caitlyn's senses flew to red-alert, and her breath came fast. "Lower your weapon," she ordered, letting the items in her hands fall to the ground.

"Easy does it, pig. I'd hate to have to shoot you, but I will."

His partner's head swiveled as he watched for trouble. "Come on, Garth. Let's just get Maisy and get out of here before somebody calls more cops."

"Unlock the doors," the one called Garth said, again.

Caitlyn held her hands, fingers spread open, in front of herself. "Okay. My key fob is on my belt. I'm just going to reach for it. No one needs to get hurt."

Garth grinned and spit on the ground between them. Caitlyn lowered her right hand and pressed the hot-pop button on her belt with her forearm. Instantly, the door of her specially fitted K9 car popped open, and Renegade sprang out, all teeth and snarls. Before the men registered what happened, Renegade bolted from the Explorer and attacked the man holding the gun. He clamped down on the man's arm before knocking him to the ground. The pistol clattered away to the curb.

Caitlyn snatched up the firearm and ran to the second man. She spun him around, slammed him against the Explorer, and in a smooth movement, reached for her cuffs and clapped them on his wrists. After checking him for weapons, she unclipped the radio from her belt and called the local police for backup.

Renegade held his man's face pressed against the concrete parking lot until Caitlyn could apprehend him. "Good boy, Ren."

When the local police arrived, she transferred custody of the men to them. The cops ignored their claims of innocence and blame. Caitlyn gave Renegade his favorite chew toy to play with as a reward for doing his job, and when he'd had enough, she returned him to his kennel.

Because of the escape attempt, Caitlyn returned Maisy Conn to the prison. The woman complained the entire drive back, screaming about police violence and abuse of power. Caitlyn was relieved she wouldn't have to listen to her rant for two long days of driving.

As she transferred custody back to the prison, Caitlyn told the intake guard, "A US Marshal will be in touch today with how they want to handle the prisoner transfer from here on out. But Ms. Conn is all yours until they decide how best to move her."

After writing an incident report and filling out the necessary forms, Caitlyn left Conn in the capable hands of the prison guards. She returned to Renegade who waited for her in the Explorer. As they left the prison grounds for the second time that morning, she called Marshal Williams to explain.

"Sounds like you've done all you can with Ms. Conn. I'll handle it from here. Would you rather head to the airport and fly to Tennessee now? Or continue to drive?"

"Honestly, ma'am, I'd rather drive. I love the hot-pop system in my car and the confidence of knowing my K9 partner is only two strides away." Caitlyn closed her eyes and swallowed. She hadn't thought for one minute she'd need the remote door popping device so soon after what happened to her last summer, but she was beyond grateful she had it.

"That's fine. Drive through to Shelbyville then and let me know when you get there."

"Will do, ma'am. Thank you." Caitlyn hung up and hugged Renegade's head that he'd poked through the small opening between his kennel and the driver's seat. He licked her cheek, and she kissed his muzzle. "You're my hero, Ren." He barked happily and wagged his tail.

A day and a half later, Caitlyn crossed the Mississippi River and drove into Memphis on her way to Shelbyville. A thin dusting of snow iced the rolling hills of the picturesque countryside and kissed the bare branches of stately trees and dark green pines. If the landscape she viewed gave any clues, she looked forward to seeing the luxurious horse farm she'd be staying at for the next week or so. This assignment was looking more and more like a vacation than work.

Caitlyn followed the GPS directions down a long country lane that took her past acres of gray-green pastures edged with dark-stained, four-rail fences, and finally led her to an impressive stone gateway. She turned between the massive pillars and drove up a tree-lined drive toward a white country mansion trimmed with black shutters and boasting spires that jutted skyward. About a hundred yards behind the house stood a massive matching barn. The tall trees were currently bereft of leaves, but their branches were thick and plentiful, and it wasn't hard to imagine how beautiful the drive and acreage must be in the summer.

She pulled up to the huge house, and as she parked, Caitlyn noticed the drapes in the front window move. After clipping Renegade's leash to his vest, they approached the imposing black lacquered double front doors. Compared to the warmth of her car, the air outside was cool, and she shivered as she rapped against the door with an elegant brass knocker shaped in the form of a horse's snaffle bit.

The woman who opened the entrance had a US Marshal's badge hanging from a chain around her neck. "You must be Deputy Reed."

"Yes, and this is my K9, Renegade." Her dog sat obediently at her side, and she stroked his head.

"Come on in. I'm Terresa Collins, and this is Phill Rodgers, and Chief Cook." She pointed to two other equally fit men wearing matching badges. "We're glad you're here. None of us have any idea what to do with those hot-headed horses out in the barn."

Caitlyn nodded to the other Deputy Marshals. "No problem. This doesn't exactly look like rough duty." She smirked as she took in her opulent surroundings. When she and Renegade stepped into the entryway rotunda, she tried hard not to gape as her gaze rose to the top of the stain-glassed spire overhead. She struggled to imagine people truly living in a home like that. The owners had decorated their mansion in warm honey-colored wood, and jewel-toned fabrics and brocades.

Collins gestured for her to follow. "I'll give you a tour while we wait for dinner. We ordered pizza. Hope that works for you."

At the mention of food, Caitlyn realized how hungry she was. "Sounds great."

"Good. Follow me. As you see, we've set up shop here in the dining room. The formal living room is across the entryway on the other side."

Caitlyn peered into the darkened room, counting four impressive equestrian paintings on the walls, each lit with their own portrait lamps. "Clearly, there's big money in horse racing."

"There can be, but we're discovering that it wasn't only winning races that built this fortune. The owner, Charles Rutledge, and his wife Tansey were also dipping their toes into gun smuggling and more recently drug dealing. Rutledge is on the run. We believe he's hiding out in Puerto Rico. However, we apprehended his wife. She's over in county lock-up for now but isn't talking."

Deputy Marshal Collins led them through the rest of the eight-bedroom house and showed Caitlyn the room where she and Ren would sleep. She then pointed out the pool, covered for the winter, and the path that led to the barn. "There are ATVs you can drive back and forth when you need to go to the barn. Do you feed horses once, or twice a day?" Collins climbed onto one of the four-wheeled vehicles and started the engine.

"Usually twice a day. Is there a schedule posted? Or any information on the horses' diets?" Caitlyn swung her leg over the seat of the second ATV. "My horses aren't anything like these beauties, and I bet they have special feed." She turned on her engine and shifted the vehicle into gear. Renegade barked at her, wagging his tail, and bouncing with excitement. "At home, he races the ATVs, and the engine sound means playtime to him." She sped past Collins, and Ren chased her down to the barn.

The sliding barn doors stood open, welcoming Caitlyn to a stunning view of the barn's breezeway bathed in warm light. She'd never seen a barn floor so clean, but what shocked her more was the number of horse stalls. She counted ten on each side, with twenty equine heads curved toward her in anticipation of dinner. "I wasn't told there were this many horses here. This is gonna be a ton of work. Is there a ranch foreman or anything? Who helps care for all of them?"

"I thought that's why you were here?" Collins cocked her head and gave her a confused look.

"Well, yeah, but one person can't manage twenty head of racing thoroughbreds on their own. The feeding alone will take over an hour, and then there's the clean-up, grooming, and turn-out. Are you sure there's no other help?" Caitlyn's awe quickly turned to overwhelm.

Collins shrugged. "I know nothing about the barn and the horses besides that the tack-room and office are through this door." She opened a door leading to a comfortable office. There was a large white board attached to one wall with each horse's name, stall number, and feeding schedule recorded.

"This helps. I'll figure it out, but I may need a couple pairs of extra hands."

"Not mine. Horses freak me out," Collins laughed. "We can ask the others if they'll help."

"According to this schedule," Caitlyn glanced at her watch, "we should have fed them an hour ago. Let's get that done before we head back to the house. You don't need to go into their stalls. Here, I'll show you." She scooped the designated feed into the first stall's grain bin, then she tossed two leaves of hay through the stall door window. "Each stall has an automatic waterer, so once they're all fed, we can go back up to the house."

A little over an hour later, they climbed back onto the ATVs and drove to the mansion. Inside, Caitlyn breathed in the scent of cheesy pizza, and she grabbed a slice on her way to collect her suitcase and Renegade's food and toys. She fed Ren his supper in the kitchen and started in on another slice of a meat-covered pie for herself.

After he finished his dinner, Deputy Marshal Rogers stood and stretched, "I've got to get to the hospital. It's my turn for guard duty tonight. I'll be transporting our witness, Bill Hayes, to the WITSEC office in the morning so he can start the process of disappearing."

"Why's he going into witness protection? Is his life in danger? I thought the bad guy left the country." Caitlyn lifted a third gooey slice from the cardboard box as Renegade curled up on the floor by her feet.

"The drug deal that our witness, Billy Hayes, was in the middle of transacting, went sideways. His partner was killed. The dealers shot Hayes too and left him for dead. We confiscated the drugs and guns, so the dealers are out the money, and Hayes can identify the shooter. So, we have a furious drug dealer who thinks Hayes is dead, but when he shows up in court to testify, the ruse will end, and Hayes will most likely lose his pitiful life if we don't hide him."

6

Early the next morning, Caitlyn and Renegade walked to the barn. This was the most beautiful equine estate she'd ever seen, even in photos. She figured it would take her an hour and a half to feed and the rest of the day to clean all the stalls.

On one hand, the work was pleasant with the impressive horses and in such an elegant and state-of-the-art barn. But on the other hand, it irked her she wasn't using any of her professional training as a deputy marshal. It didn't take a genius to feed and care for horses, after all. She'd been doing this work since she was a kid. She understood that these fancy racehorses needed someone with experience, especially if anything went wrong, but Caitlyn wanted to do the work of a US Deputy Marshal, not that of a farm hand.

Renegade trotted behind her from stall to stall, his tail waving in the air as she measured out each horse's specific grain rations. Then Caitlyn attached a wagon loaded with hay bales to an ATV and drove down the row, tossing leaves into each stall. When she finished, she breathed in the dried, green scent of the grass and closed her eyes to listen to the horses munching.

The sound reminded her of home and the times she sat with Colt drinking a cold beer and listening to that particular music in the evenings, after the work was done. The rhythmic crunching normally settled in her soul and assured her all was right in the world. But these racers were high-strung and hot headed, so as soon as they finished eating, she turned most of them out to the pastures where they could burn off their excess energy.

Caitlyn leaned against a gate and savored several peaceful minutes of watching the beautiful four-legged creatures run and prance, tossing their heads while they flagged their tails high behind them. They reminded her of deer or gazelles. Compared to her family's ranch horses, these thoroughbreds were like equine super models. She smirked at the thought and went into the barn to find a muck rake.

She started on the first stall and had her back to the door when Renegade jumped to his feet and barked. Caitlyn's heartbeat flared and her chest tightened as she spun around, pointing the tines of her fork toward a short man who had entered the barn. "Who are you?"

The slight man stood about five feet tall and couldn't have weighed much more than a hundred pounds. He froze when he saw Renegade, and his gaze bounced between Caitlyn and her dog. "Whoa, you two. It's okay, I'm friendly." Her reaction had obviously surprised him, but he grinned, and openly gave Caitlyn a full once over.

"I'm Danny Franco. I work here. Who are you, sweet-heart? Are you new?"

"In a matter of speaking." She glared at Danny. "What do you do here? Exercise the horses?" She assumed so because of his size.

"That's right. And I jockey for Mr. Rutledge on occa-sion, too. In fact, I have a race coming up next week."

"Not anymore, you don't."

"What? Why not? Where's Mr. Rutledge?" Danny glanced toward the barn office door.

"A few things have come up. Tell me, when did you last see Charles Rutledge?"

Danny studied Caitlyn for a minute before he answered. "Last week. Maybe ten days ago, or so. He's not always here. I haven't been to the barn since early last week. Me and my family changed apartments and I've been moving our stuff. Why?" He shot his gaze around the stables. "Is he okay? Did something happen to him? Who are you, by the way?" Dark brows crunched over warm brown eyes.

Caitlyn lowered the fork tines to the floor. "I'm Deputy Marshal Caitlyn Reed. We've seized the Rutledge's property. I'm here to make sure these animals are cared for until we find Mr. Rutledge, who is currently missing."

"Missing? And what do you mean, seized the proper-ty?" Danny crossed his arms over his chest. "Has some-thing happened to Mr. Rutledge? What about Tansey—uh —Mrs. Rutledge? Is she here?"

"Not at the moment." Caitlyn watched Danny for signs of nerves or defensiveness but only saw genuine confusion. "Hey, since you're employed by the Rutledge's, why don't you help me finish cleaning out the stalls?"

He sent her an incredulous look. "I don't muck manure. I ride. And by the way, we never turn all these horses out together at the same time. They could get hurt —and I'm guessing you don't have a million bucks to replace any of them if they do."

"Don't worry. I kept the stallions in their stalls. I'm not an idiot. But the mares seem to get along, and they needed to stretch their legs. I'm assuming no one has let them out since the last time you were here. How long did you say that was? A week? Ten days?"

"That's right. No one's been here? What about the grooms? The vet? This place is usually hopping." Danny peered out at the mares who had settled down and were grazing in the field.

"Was someone feeding them, at least?" His concern seemed real to Caitlyn, so she gave him the benefit of the doubt.

"Yes, but that's about all. I don't think anyone has exercised them, turned them out, or cleaned up after them for several days." She scooped a fork full of horse apples and tossed the pile into a manure spreader she'd attached to the ATV.

Danny jumped out of the way. "I guess I could help— since there's no one else here—but I want to know what's going on."

"For now, why don't you go on up to the house. There are a few marshals up there who'll want to talk to you. When they're done with their questions, if they say it's okay, you can come back down here. You probably should ride the stallions and burn off some of their energy."

"But why are Federal Marshals here? What's going on?" Danny stepped toward Caitlyn and Renegade growled at his intrusion. The small man stopped in his tracks. "Is this your dog?"

"Yes. He's my K9 partner, and it sounds like he doesn't want you coming any closer to me." Caitlyn leaned on the fork. Allowing Danny to remain uncomfortable, she told Ren he was a good boy. "You'll find out more about the situation when you talk to the marshals at the house."

"Okay. I'll be back in a while, then."

Caitlyn chuckled. "I hope so. I sure as hell don't want to do all this by myself."

Danny left, and as he walked toward the double sliding barn doors, he raised his hand in farewell.

After his interview with the local marshals, Danny returned to the barn. He took the stallions through their paces, then helped Caitlyn tidy up the remaining stalls. Working side by side with Caitlyn, the jockey gradually earned Renegade's approval.

Danny tossed a forkful of manure into the spreader. "After we're done here, I still need to run a couple of those mares."

"Sounds good." Caitlyn's lumbar muscles ached. She was used to this type of work, but not the amount, and her back complained. Twisting side to side to loosen her lower vertebrae, she said, "Thanks for helping. If we stay on top of it from here on out, it won't be so bad."

"How long before the grooms come back?" Danny

tossed a shovel full of manure and spent wood shavings into the wagon.

"I'm not sure. I'm not lead on this case. Honestly, I'm just here to take care of the animals and guard the place at night."

The Tennessee marshals assigned to the case left the property in the late afternoon, stopping by the barn to inform Caitlyn that a team of admin workers would arrive in the morning to inventory all the items in the house. After they drove away, Danny pressed for more information.

"Why are they doing an inventory?"

"The USMS seized the estate and will sell it all at auction. That includes all the stuff inside, and everything out here. Horses and all."

"You're kidding! What for? Does this mean I don't have a job anymore?" Danny tossed his shovel onto the floor. "I've got kids—a family. I need this job!" He kicked a pile of manure and sent it scattering across the stall.

"I'm sorry. Maybe the government will pay you to stay on until the sales are final. We could use your help."

"Then what?"

"I don't know. I'm sure there are other race farms that need exercise jockeys."

"You don't understand. I've worked my way up here. I've been exercising horses here for years, and I was finally getting my chance to race. Now, I'll have to start all over again!"

Caitlyn didn't know what to say. There were no words that would make this any easier for him. They finished their barn chores in silence, and while Danny exercised the few still-antsy mares by running laps around the track, Caitlyn brought the other horses back inside for their evening feeding.

IT WAS SHAPING up to be another long, trying day of rural sheriffing. Colt's first call that morning was from two neighbors arguing about each other's dogs trespassing on their respective farms. It didn't matter that the families had been friends for the past thirty years, or that the dogs were littermates, or that they'd frequented each other's properties every day up to then. Today, they caught the dogs digging up bulbs in one of the flower gardens. Both animals were at fault, but the offended property owner demanded restitution from his neighbor for the destruction.

Colt pointed out that the bulbs were unharmed and ended up replanting them in the frozen ground himself to put an end to the loud argument. When the work was done, the neighbors clapped each other on the back and disappeared inside to share a hot toddy. Colt, cold and grumpy, blasted the heat in his Jeep on his way back to the office.

After lunch, he'd spent the afternoon researching his rights as a parent and going over all the details of attaining 50/50 parenting time. His biggest takeaway was that he needed to get everything set in stone through the court, and it was imperative that he did that before Allison got it in her mind to leave the state. If she did, he'd have hell to pay trying to get the time he wanted with

Jace. He'd end up only seeing his son at Christmas and in the summer, and he wasn't about to let that happen.

As it was, Allison wanted to move out of her parents' house, but didn't have the income to afford a decent place on her own. Colt hadn't much time. He couldn't speed up the court, but he could provide a place for Allison and Jace to live. He'd call Caitlyn after work to discuss which house the two of them were going to settle in. Whichever one they decided on, he'd offer the other to Allison.

Colt's phone rang. It was Wes. "I was just about to head home. What's up?"

"I'm out at the Adams's place. They have two dead cows in their pasture. They say it happened suddenly."

"That's two ranches reporting dead cows this week." Colt ran his hand down the back of his neck. "Did Adams say he noticed any prior symptoms? Did he call the vet?"

"The vet is on his way."

"Good. Well, stay there until he gets there, then let me know what he says."

"Sounds good."

"I'll be at home if you need me. You're on call tonight, right?"

"Yes, sir."

"Okay. Keep me posted."

Colt twisted a scarf around his neck and pulled on his heavy Carhartt jacket. On the way to his Jeep, he considered what might be killing the local cattle. It was bitter cold in northern Wyoming in January, but they hadn't had any unusual weather for this time of year. Maybe the cows weren't getting enough water. Or it could be tainted feed... but wouldn't that affect an entire herd?

He'd talk to Dr. Moore in the morning. He'd give Jim Miller, over at the feed store, a call too. Maybe the owners of the dead cattle all purchased the same supplements or something.

The jeep's engine sputtered to life in the frigid evening, and Colt scraped ice from the windshield while he let the motor warm up. It was only six o'clock, but the sun had gone to bed a while ago. Colt decided to stay at his house in town for the night and looked forward to spending the rest of the evening in front of a warm fire with a thick steak.

His house was only a couple of blocks from the office and within minutes he pulled into the driveway. He hadn't even put the Jeep in park before his phone rang.

"This is Tammy in dispatch. Sorry to bother you, Sheriff, but Deputy Cooper is on another call. I got a 911 call from Tom Williams. He says some kids are out TP-ing his trees."

"Seriously? That's not an emergency. Can't he just open the door and holler at them?" Colt shifted into reverse.

"Sorry, Sheriff. I just pass on the calls. Tom sounded pretty angry, so maybe it's better if he doesn't yell at them."

Colt sighed as his jeep bounced into the street. So much for that juicy steak. "I'm on my way. Thanks, Tammy."

"Stay warm tonight."

"I'll try." Colt turned toward the side of town where the Williamses lived. Dogs... kids... cows... was settling petty disputes and solving the deaths of ranch animals going to be his lot in life? When he dreamed of becoming a sheriff, he had something far more exciting in mind.

As soon as he pulled to the curb in front of the Williamses' house, the perpetrators of tissue vandalism scattered. Colt wasn't about to chase any of them down. A red-faced Tom met him on the front porch.

"Did you see them, Sheriff? Look at this mess. Who's going to clean this up?" Williams gestured at his trees, bare of leaves but draped in white. "What do you plan to do about it?"

"It's hardly a serious crime, Tom. Weren't you ever a kid?"

Williams looked askance. "Of course, I was a kid. One that respected other people's property."

"I'm sure." Colt cleared the sarcasm out of his throat. He noticed the Williamses' high-school-aged daughter watching them from the front window. "Didn't your daughter make the Winter Dance Royalty Court recently?"

Tom puffed up, and a smile cut across his face. "Why yes, she did. Did you see her picture in the paper?"

"Yes. Did you know that it's a long-standing tradition to TP the homes of those on the royalty court? Hell, Tom, they've been doing that around here since I was in high school."

"They have?" The man blinked and panned his gaze across his yard.

Colt played to Tom's ego. "Look at it as a symbol of your daughter's popularity. Folks who drive by will know she's a winter dance princess."

"Then, I should leave it?"

"Up to you. Or you could get your daughter out here and the two of you could clean it up. Shouldn't take too long."

"Well, it's awfully cold right now. Maybe I'll leave it for a warmer day."

"Good thinking." Colt stuffed his icy fingers in his coat pockets. "If that's all, I'll be saying good night, then."

"Good night, Sheriff. And thank you—you know—for telling me."

"Not a problem. Now, get inside where it's warm." Colt turned on his heel and rushed back to the warmth of his Jeep. It was times like this he thought being Sheriff was more like being a politician—smoothing feathers and kissing babies—than keeping the law.

When he got home, Colt started a fire in the hearth and pan-fried his steak. He had no desire to go back out in the cold to start the grill on the deck. He settled himself in front of the TV to watch the Avalanche - Edmonton Oilers hockey game and clicked the FaceTime app on his phone to call Caitlyn. Isolation pressed heavy on his chest with each ring that went unanswered.

7

***

When Danny left for home at the end of the long day, Caitlyn and Renegade returned to the mansion for the night. She was worn out, so after a quick bite of dinner, Caitlyn lit a fire in the fireplace and she and Ren settled in to watch some TV. She drifted off to sleep with the lullaby of canned sitcom-laughter.

Hours later, Caitlyn flew to her feet from a dead sleep at the jarring sound of Renegade barking and snarling at the back door. She sucked in a breath and reached for the Glock holstered at her side. Blood pounded in her head and adrenaline zipped through her body. She crouched next to Renegade and peered outside around the edge of the door trying to see what had so upset her dog. Renegade maintained his frantic alert.

"Good boy, Ren. What is it? Is someone out there?" A light flashed inside the barn. "Ren, *kemne*," she commanded as she silently slid the glass door open. Renegade quieted and followed her outside. As they crept toward the barn, Caitlyn heard harshly whispered voices on the breeze and the sound of stall doors clanging. She and Renegade skirted the south side of the barn. They were approaching the far end of the structure when a truck engine roared. Tires spit gravel and the bright red taillights of a horse trailer bounced down the road, signaling its escape.

Caitlyn pointed her gun at the fleeing truck and yelled for the driver to stop. A figure in the rear seat of the crew cab leaned out the window, aimed a rifle, and shot at her. She wanted to return fire but held back, afraid of hitting the horses in the trailer. Instead, she dove to the shadowed ground. Renegade chased after the rig. Caitlyn screamed for him to come back. The gunman fired two more rounds.

Dirt and rocks bit into her skin, and Renegade yelped. "Ren!" Caitlyn scurried across the drive to her dog as the truck disappeared into the night. "Were you hit?" Her hands flew over his body and limbs. Renegade licked her fingers as she confirmed for herself that he was unharmed. He'd likely yipped when the flying gravel hit his face.

Relieved that both she and Ren came through the incident uninjured, Caitlyn reached for her phone and called 911 to report the theft and shooting. Next, she dialed her local supervisor. Within twenty minutes the property was fully lit with floods and red, white, and blue lights flashing around the house and barn. She gave the officers a situation report while the crime scene investigators dusted for prints, gathered shell casings, and searched for stray bullets.

The EMT on location insisted on taking her vitals and attempted to guide her to the ambulance.

"I'm fine," she grumbled.

"You have several scratches and a cut on your face. At least let me tend to those."

Caitlyn opened her mouth to argue when she saw the speculative gaze of her supervisor watching her. "Fine but make it quick."

She sat in the back of the ambulance while the paramedic cleaned her scrapes and applied a butterfly bandage to a small laceration on her forehead. "I'm required to check your vitals, ma'am. It won't take more than a couple of minutes. You don't want me to get in trouble, do you?" He grinned and winked. Quickly, before she had another chance to resist, he slid a blood pressure cuff around her arm and pressed his stethoscope to her wrist. While he listened, he peered into her eyes, and she breathed deeply hoping to slow her racing heart rate.

The auto-cuff relaxed, and he wrote the numbers on a record sheet. "Your blood pressure is higher than I like to see. Even after a stressful event such as this. And your pupils are dilated. I want you to come into the ER for a full exam. Better safe than sorry."

"I told you, I'm fine," Caitlyn snapped and hopped to her feet. "I'm probably just experiencing a little shock."

"Yes, and I'd like you to lie down. I can give you an IV to help." He touched her shoulder. "Please?"

"It's not surprising I'm showing signs of stress. Someone just shot at me. But they missed, so I'm okay." She stepped away but turned back. "Thanks, though, and I promise I'll come in if I feel any worse. Alright?"

The paramedic shrugged. "Your call, but at least drink some water." He handed her a plastic bottle.

She sucked the water down all at once and smiled at him. "Thanks, I needed that."

He shook his head and tossed her a second bottle. "Get some rest, stay hydrated, and take care of yourself."

"Will do. Thanks." The team of marshals had congregated up at the house. Caitlyn called to Ren, and they hurried to join them.

COLT'S PHONE rang in the middle of a tropical dream. He and Caitlyn were walking hand in hand on a white-sand beach, somewhere. Without opening his eyes, he felt around the nightstand for his phone. It better not be another TP-tattling. "Yeah? This is Branson."

"Colt? Sorry to wake you, but I'd want you to call me if—"

He sat up in bed, suddenly fully awake. "Catie? What's wrong? Are you okay?"

"Yes, I'm fine." Caitlyn recounted the night's events and reassured him several times over the loud pounding of his heart, that neither she nor Renegade had been hurt. "I just needed to hear your voice."

"You can call me anytime. But I thought this was supposed to be a babysitting type of assignment, and now you're getting shot at. I think you should come home."

"What? Why?" Indignation filled her tone. "I'm not coming home. I have a job to do."

Colt sighed and rubbed his eyes with the heel of his hand. "I know. It's just that…"

"You still don't believe I'm ready to be back on the job." She sounded disappointed, spurring Colt's conscience.

"No, I do. I know you're great at your job, and if you say you're ready, then you are. I think maybe I'm the one who's not ready. I almost lost you last summer, Catie."

"But you didn't. We both have risky jobs. We knew that going in."

Colt scoffed. His job was anything *but* dangerous… lately. If he was honest with himself, he'd have to admit that he was a little envious of Caitlyn's work. "You're right. I know. I'm glad you called." He turned on his bedside lamp and stuffed a pillow behind his back. "Since I have you on the phone, can we talk about our housing situation?"

"What about it?"

"When I saw Allison yesterday, she said she wants to move out of her parents' house. But she can't afford anywhere around here, and she talked about taking Jace back to Missouri again. I can't let her do that. If she leaves Wyoming before I get a court-ordered parenting agreement, I'm hosed. I won't ever get regular parenting time."

"Do you think she'd do that?"

"Who knows, but I don't want to take the chance." Colt took a breath and risked pitching his idea. "So, I was thinking, maybe they could move into the cabin, and we could live here in town."

Silence screamed over the phone.

"Catie?"

"Look, Colt," Caitlyn's voice was low and steely. "I've

been as amenable as I can, but there is no way I'm giving up my cabin so Allison Snow can live there. No way in hell. You can do whatever you want with your house, but I'm keeping mine."

He'd pissed her off, and now she was ticking him off too. None of this was for Allison—it was for Jace. Couldn't she see that? Didn't she care? Admittedly, it was stupid of him to bring the issue up in the middle of the night, and now he wanted to end the conversation before things got any worse, but he didn't resist a parting shot. "I thought we gave up 'mine and yours' when we got married."

"Yeah, well, I thought there'd only be one woman in your life you cared about pleasing. Guess we were both wrong." The line went dead.

8

Caitlyn couldn't sleep. She hadn't been fair to Colt on the phone, but it was beyond belief that he had asked her to give up *their* cabin to Allison. Besides, the house in town would be much more convenient for the woman and Jace. Of course, she understood the house was closer to Colt's work too, especially if he got called out in the middle of the night.

"Ugh!" she growled and covered her head with a pillow. Renegade poked her bare arm with his cold nose. "It's okay, Ren. I'm just mad."

Morning came too soon, and Caitlyn dragged herself into the shower. She didn't want to call Colt until she was no longer angry, so she filled Renegade's bowl with kibble and sucked down a strong cup of coffee while he ate. The day started early on the farm and wanting their breakfast, the horses whinnied at her as she and Ren made their way to the barn.

"Coming, coming! Hold your horses." She laughed at the ridiculousness of the pun. "Be patient!"

The two empty stalls at the far end of the barn brought a vivid recollection of the previous night's theft. Caitlyn would much rather be chasing the thieves than be stuck doing barn chores. She had graduated at the top of her class at the Federal Law Enforcement Training Center and the USMS Academy, and for what? To muck stalls? She'd been doing that her whole life. Caitlyn plunged the metal scoop into the grain bin harder than necessary.

Even though it was mindless work that took no skill, there was simply too much of it to do on her own. She had asked the Nashville's Chief Deputy to consider hiring Danny to help her. The sale of one horse would more than pay for his annual salary—and hers.

The would-be jockey arrived shortly after she started with the grain. Having decided Danny was a friend, Renegade greeted him with a cheerful bark. He patted Ren on the head before following Caitlyn down the stable row with the hay rations. "Where are the two horses on the end? Their stall doors are open." Danny ran to the side door to look out at the track.

"They're not out there. Somebody broke in last night and stole them. There was a shoot-out and everything. You missed all the excitement."

"What? Was anyone hurt?" Shock widened his eyes, and he gave her a once over. "You have a cut on your face."

Caitlyn absently touched the bandage above her eyebrow. "I'm fine. Some flying gravel hit me, that's all. Thankfully, the horse thieves were terrible shots. The vet is due out this morning to check on the other horses. Just to be safe." She scooped the last serving of grain into a black horse's bin.

Danny's face paled. "They *shot* at you?" He cocked his head when a chestnut horse poked his nose out of his stall near the end of the row. "Triton?"

"You seem surprised to see him."

Scratching his chin, Danny nodded. "I am. I mean, he's the fastest horse in the barn. You'd think the horse thieves would have taken him."

"They probably just grabbed whoever was closest to the door. Either way, it can't be a coincidence that the owner skips town and then someone shows up to steal his horses."

"I'm sure it isn't. Mr. Rutledge owed some questionable men a lot of money."

Caitlyn turned to study Danny's face. "Do you know who those men are?"

Danny shrugged. "Not by name. I know he was afraid of a man he called The Banker."

"The Banker? Was he a loan-shark?"

"I guess, maybe. Mr. Rutledge never talked to me directly about it. I only know what I've heard."

Caitlyn sat on a bale of hay and scratched Renegade's ears. "What else have you heard?"

"Just that Rutledge needed money. Things were going south with the farm. It's why he was letting me race. He could afford me because he would only pay me a percentage of the purse—if I won."

Caitlyn glanced over the pristine facility. "Everything looks in good condition around here. Why do you think your boss needed money? Couldn't he just sell a horse, or something?"

"Maybe he needed more than that. There were whispers about him being in trouble with the IRS."

"Interesting." Caitlyn stood and stretched. "I'm going to get started on that inventory list in the barn office. Do you mind finishing up here before you exercise the horses?"

"I'm on it." Danny whistled as he finished tossing hay.

Caitlyn patted Ren's side. "Come on, boy. We have some ciphering to do." She led the way to the office, but instead of filling out an inventory sheet, she turned on the farm's desktop PC. It had the same password as the system up at the house, which made her job easier. After a quick search, she located the barn's financial ledgers. Even at first glance, she knew the numbers differed from the ones recorded on the main computer.

Caitlyn studied the inventory lists. The books stated there should be sixty tons of hay in the hay shed and 110 bags of grain. She could tell by looking, that the grass they had didn't come anywhere near sixty tons, so she dashed to the feed room and counted sacks. There were twenty-three. Caitlyn recorded the discrepancy on a new spread-sheet. She suspected Rutledge's business was on the brink of bankruptcy and that he, or someone, had been tweaking these records as well as the household accounts. These numbers presented a whole new bundle of tax fraud evidence. Add this to last night's horse theft and getting shot at... no way was she walking away from this case, no matter how Colt felt about it.

Ren got to his feet and stared at the office door wagging his tail, so it didn't surprise Caitlyn when Danny entered. "Have you talked to your boss about me keeping my job here? I only ask cuz I'm scheduled to race next

Thursday. I could take a cut of my winnings and the barn could keep the rest. Seems like a win-win deal to me. It's gonna cost the Marshals Service to feed these beasts before they auction them off, you know?"

"I asked, but I haven't heard yet. I don't see any reason they wouldn't agree to it, though. I need your help, for sure. As far as the racing goes, aren't there entry fees and stall fees? Besides, why are you so certain you'll win?"

"I'll win cuz I *gotta* win. I'm counting on that money." Desperation laced his voice. "I've got to feed my family— keep a roof over their heads, you know?" Danny reached for his wallet and pulled out several school photos of his children—two adorable boys with their father's nose. "Ya gotta help me, Caitlyn."

"I'll do what I can. I promise." Caitlyn's phone rang, and she checked the screen. Dirk's dark eyes glowered back at her. "I gotta take this." She answered the call and walked outside for some privacy. "Sterling, you calling to tell me you've finally got Trova snuggled up in a cell?"

"Unfortunately, no."

"No? What happened? I thought all you had to do was scoop him up."

"That was the plan, but at the last minute, the goombah decided to mark off a bucket list item and go on a road trip with a friend."

"Where?"

"That's the question of the hour. We're not sure if he's left New York yet, but apparently, he bought a brand new, top-end, luxury RV to drive south in."

"That shouldn't be hard to track."

"Not if he registered it legally and all, but this is

Anthony Trova we're talking about. We think he's already on the road, possibly headed toward Florida, and we've alerted the state police along the direct route. But on the chance he's still in New York somewhere, we're driving back out to his estate on Long Island to poke around. How are things going down on the horse farm?"

Caitlyn told him about the theft the night before.

"See? And you were worried you'd miss out on all the excitement. You're the one getting shot at, while I'm chasing a couple of geriatric wise-guys in a lux RV."

Caitlyn laughed at the image. "Just remember, he may look like a harmless older man, but he's a stone-cold killer. Be vigilant."

"Will do. You watch your six too."

"I've got Renegade for that."

9

Deputy Chief Cook stopped by the horse farm for an informal meeting. He told the team he wanted to catch up on the details of the case and hear firsthand from Caitlyn about the horse theft the night before. After she filled him in on all she knew, including the creative accounting she discovered in the ledgers in the barn office, she told him about Danny.

"Personally, I need his help with the horse-related chores. Twenty—well, eighteen now—high-maintenance racehorses are too many for one person to care for. Especially these hot-blooded thoroughbreds. They require daily exercise to stay in shape and sane."

The director cocked his head to the side. "What are we talking here, Reed? Minimum wage? Full time? Hiring a stable hand isn't in my budget."

"I think it's only fair that we offer him what he's accustomed to. It might not matter to you, but with his help we can maintain these horses' value and get what they're worth at the auction. Plus, Danny's already registered to race in the upcoming regional races. We could pay him from his winnings… if he wins or even if he merely places."

"Wait just one minute, Reed. The USMS is not in the horse racing business. We aren't here to make money. We're here to catalog inventory and then auction it off. That includes all those high-strung horses out there."

"I know that sir, but Danny's certain he can win, and the purse would easily reimburse the marshals service for the entry fee, stall rental, and his salary." Caitlyn held her breath waiting for the explosion she knew would happen.

"Are you kidding me?" the director's voice rose. "Now you want my office to pay for this wanna-be jockey to race, too? Not a chance!"

"Come on, sir. I think we should consider Danny a victim of Rutledge's crimes. He's an innocent third party. Don't we allot a portion of our asset forfeiture to compensate victims? Besides, I have a secondary motive for Danny to enter the race. It gives us a reason to be in the race stables where we could gain some intel on the horse theft. The local track is the best place to hear any gossip about that. If we catch the horse thieves, they could lead us to Rutledge. Not to mention, with what those horses are worth we could bring the perps up on felony theft charges if we arrest them." Caitlyn fisted her hands at her sides, willing her body to hold still.

"Since Rutledge is missing, his horses haven't been officially reported as stolen. So, I suppose it's *possible* that they might be entered into some races." Cook tapped his fingers on the counter while he spoke. He was considering all the angles, but if he didn't agree to fund her racing idea, Caitlyn had decided to back Danny herself with her personal savings. It was risky, but Danny had shown her Triton's speed record. He was sure they could win, and so was she.

Colt's face floated across her mind's eye. Her new husband would probably blow a gasket if he knew what she was considering. Would she ever grow accustomed to thinking in terms of the two of them and not just herself?

The director stared her in the eye, and she held his gaze without blinking. Finally, he said, "Tell me, Deputy Reed, what's this horse's average speed on the furlong?"

"DANNY! WHERE ARE YOU?" Caitlyn and Renegade ran out to the barn. Elegant equine faces poked through the openings in the stall doors to see who was yelling. "Danny!" she called again. She leaned in through the office door, but he wasn't there, so she sprinted out the side doors and up the pathway to the practice track on the south side of the stables. The jockey's form bobbed up and down, floating above the far-side rail of the oval astride Triton, the chestnut stallion he wanted for the upcoming race. She braced her forearms against the white fence. "*Lehne.*" At her soft-spoken command, Renegade lay down next to her. Within seconds, the horse and rider flew by them, spraying a mist of sand as they passed.

After they crossed the finish line, Danny slowed his mount for a cool-down lap. On the backside of the track, he eased Triton into an extended trot and returned to where Caitlyn stood. "He feels fantastic. He'd have gone even faster if I'd have let him. Imagine if he had the pressure of competition spurring him on!"

"You two look amazing together. And guess what? You won't have to imagine his ultimate speed for long."

Danny's face went blank for a second as he thought about what she said, but when the realization hit him, his eyes glowed with excitement. "Are you serious? I have a job? I get to race?"

Triton pranced sideways under Danny's excited energy, and Renegade leapt up to join in the fun. "*Sedni*, Ren." Caitlyn admonished affectionately. "The last thing we need is you chasing our new jockey and his racehorse across the Tennessee countryside."

"I can't believe it! Thank you, Caitlyn. Thank you! My family thanks you." Danny jumped down from Triton's back. He looked tiny standing next to the tall horse. With tears in his eyes, he hugged Caitlyn. "You've saved my family."

"I don't think it's as dramatic as all that." Heat crawled up Caitlyn's neck, and her skin itched at his gushing. "And you better win!"

"We will! Did you see him? Could you feel Triton's passion to run?"

Caitlyn laughed at Danny's exuberance. "He looked incredibly powerful." She reached up and stroked the beautiful horse's strong, sleek neck.

Danny's phone buzzed from inside his jersey. He unzipped his jacket and glanced at the screen. His smile faltered and a haunted expression she couldn't decipher swept across his features. "Do you mind hand-walking

Triton to cool him down? I've got to take this call." He handed Triton's reins to Caitlyn.

"Shouldn't I saddle up a cool-down buddy?" Caitlyn figured it would take a couple of laps around the track to fully cool the hot and sweaty racehorse and she'd need a horse to ride alongside him. "What about his sweat sheet?"

"I'll get you a second horse and the blanket after I take this call, but for now please keep Triton moving."

Caitlyn told Renegade to stay, and she dipped under the railing. She found it hard to walk in the deep sand of the track as the amped-up Triton trotted sideways, practically in place beside her. She sensed his desire to run pulsing through his veins. Renegade whined as she walked away from where she'd told him to stay. "You're a good boy, Ren," she called over her shoulder. "I'll be right back." She led the elegant chestnut to the next post and then turned back.

Renegade had circled and now sat with his back to her. His ears perked and his body tensed as he watched something near the barn. Caitlyn shifted her gaze to follow his. When she approached her dog, she saw what held his attention. Danny was on the far side of the barn talking to a man next to a black truck. She could see that the man's hands were balled up and he was shouting, but they were too far away for her to hear what was being said. Danny held out his arms in a helpless gesture and the man shook a fist at him. Renegade growled.

"I hear you, Ren. I wonder what that's all about." The man returned to his truck and sped away. Danny clapped the back of his head and lowered his chin. He shuffled back inside the barn. Eventually, he walked up the path to where they stood waiting. "Hey, you forgot to bring me another horse and Triton's sheet."

Distracted, Danny answered, "Oh, yeah. Sorry. I'll take him." He reached out for Triton's reins, but Caitlyn held onto them.

"Who was that man in the truck you were talking to?"

Danny appeared startled. He turned his gaze toward the spot where he'd been talking, and his cheeks darkened. "Oh... that. That was nobody. Just somebody asking for directions."

10

C olt dragged himself through another average day of small town sheriffing, looking forward to spending the afternoon and evening with Jace. He checked in on the local businesses on Main Street, wrote two parking tickets and pulled an out-of-towner over for speeding. He texted Caitlyn an apology for not being more sensitive to her feelings about Allison and the cabin. She hadn't answered, and Colt chose not to take it personally. It wasn't unusual for her not to respond to texts when she was working. He'd call her after he took Jace back home that night.

Wes got to the office at three for the late shift. "Hey, boss." He hung his hat and coat by the door. "Anything going on I should be aware of?"

"Nope. Usual things. News says we might get more snow tonight, so I'd expect a few cars off the road, but hopefully folks will just stay home."

Wes pulled a Coke from the mini fridge. "Want one?" He held a can toward Colt.

Colt shook his head as he texted Allison to see if he could come by early to get Jace. It had been a particularly boring day. Nothing was going on, so he put the files he was working on in the cabinet. "I'm heading out. Call me if you need me."

Wes slid into his chair. "Will do. Stay warm out there."

Colt drove to the Snows' house and waited outside on the porch while Jace got ready. Allison didn't invite him in. The late afternoon sun was too weak to help the sub-freezing day feel any warmer, so when Jace ran out of his grandparent's house with only a sweatshirt on, Colt called him back.

"It'll be bitter cold as soon as the sun goes down. You'd better get your winter coat, a hat, and some gloves. We'll be spending time outside when we're at the ranch."

Allison shivered and hugged herself as she held open the storm door. "Outside? At the Reeds' ranch? That's not a good idea, Colt. It's freezing."

"A little cold never hurt anyone." Colt stepped aside to let his son back inside the house. "Besides, I want to teach Jace how to ride."

"Today? In this weather?" Allison raised a skeptical eyebrow and shook her head. She let out a long-suffering breath and said, "Come inside while you wait. We're letting all the heat out."

The first thing they did when Colt and Jace got to the ranch was to look for Dylan and McKenzie in the newly built kennel. They found them in the office. "Wow, you've done a ton of work in here since I was here last. Jace wanted to see the dogs before I give him a riding lesson."

McKenzie rubbed her arms. "Isn't it too cold to ride?"

Dylan chuffed. "You didn't seem to think so when I rode out to work this morning."

"Yes, I did. That's why I brought you the thermos of coffee." She smiled up at her husband and leaned into him. Dylan kissed her head and then touching her chin, lifted her face so he could kiss her lips.

Their intimacy made Colt's chest ache with missing Caitlyn. He cleared his throat. "Let's keep it G-rated, okay?" He laughed as Jace's lip curled in disgust, and Colt playfully nudged his son. "We still have a couple hours of daylight, but we won't ride for long. Kenzie promised us a warm supper at six." He glanced up at McKenzie. "Mind if we go check out the pups?"

"Not at all." She pointed the way. "In fact, I'd appreciate you playing with them for a little while, Jace. It's good for their socialization. Do you mind?"

"Are you kidding?" Jace raced ahead of them to the area McKenzie kept the puppies. Huddled together, the Malinois pups napped inside a large fenced-in pen. The little dogs perked up when Jace got there. Stretching, they yipped with excitement and ran to the boy when he entered the gate, each vying for his total attention.

"Don't let them chew on you, Jace. Tell them no if they try." McKenzie grinned as she watched Colt's boy with her dogs.

"They're getting big. Are these last two sold?" Colt asked.

"Yes," wistfulness entered her voice. "They'll be gone next week." McKenzie leaned against the chain-link. "I'm going to miss them."

"I bet. When do you expect to have more?"

"I'll breed Athena after her next heat cycle, so summertime I hope."

Dylan called to Colt from the kennel office. "I'm headed to the barn, want me to tack up a horse for Jace?"

"No, thanks. I'd like him to learn how to do that for himself from the beginning," Colt answered. "We'll be there in a few minutes."

Dylan nodded and winked at his bride before he strode from the building.

"When Jace is done playing with the dogs, I'll head into the house and get dinner started. What do you hear from Caitlyn?"

Colt pursed his mouth. "Well, there was a robbery at the barn she's tending. Shots were fired." McKenzie's eyes widened and he held up his hand. "Don't worry, everyone is okay but leave it to Catie to find trouble." He chuckled, though he didn't truly see any humor in the situation.

"For sure." McKenzie peered into his eyes. "Are you doing okay?"

"With her being shot at? Hell no. But Catie dutifully reminded me that this was her job."

McKenzie grinned. "Sounds like the Reed family trait of stubbornness shining through."

"You said it." Colt shrugged out of his jacket. "How's married life treating you and Dylan?"

Her cheeks blushed a becoming soft pink. "It's great."

"Hear anymore from that Tony guy?"

"Yes, in fact. He's coming to get his two pups next week."

Colt nodded. "I met him at your wedding. He seems

like a good man. Once he accepted the fact that you were determined to marry Dylan, that is."

"He is. And he's a good cop. After seeing Athena's puppies, and since we have a history of training together, Tony said he'd buy his K9s exclusively from our kennel, and that he'd recommend us to other police departments, too."

"That's awesome. That will give you a great start."

"Yeah, and after Logan brought his boss, Clay Jennings, up at Christmas time, he said they'd check our stock first before going anywhere else. And Clay promised to recommend me to the FBI K9 training facility in Quantico, too!"

"Sounds like you're on your way, then."

"Yep." McKenzie glanced up at him. "Speaking of old flames, I heard Blake and Kayla broke up."

"I heard that too." Colt kept his gaze trained on Jace. He wasn't about to show any reaction to McKenzie's not-so-subtle prodding even though he deserved her needling after he brought up Tony. "Come on, buddy," he called to Jace. "We better get to riding if we want to be done before dark."

Jace glanced over his shoulder at his dad. "I wish I could keep one of these puppies."

"I know. But your grandparents don't want a dog, bud."

"Yeah, I guess." Jace's disappointment showed all over his body as he stood with slumped shoulders and said goodbye to the puppies.

"Thank your Aunt McKenzie."

"She's my aunt?" Jace peered up at Colt.

"Well, sort of. Yeah."

McKenzie slid her arm around the boy's shoulders. "I'd love it if you called me Aunt McKenzie! Now go have fun. Dinner will be ready when you are."

Colt buttoned his coat before heading outside with Jace on his heels. They crossed the yard to the barn. Dylan had a propane heater going in the tack room, but it was still cold. The small space smelled of leather and saddle soap. Colt stomped his feet to get his blood moving. "I think the temperature has dropped since we got here."

"Better get a move on, then. I brought Bingo up for Jace. He's ready to be groomed and tacked."

"Thanks. He's the perfect horse to learn on."

Colt pointed to a grooming bucket filled with curry combs, brushes, and hoof picks. "Grab the supplies and I'll show you how to get your horse ready to saddle."

Dylan opened Sampson's stall where his horse stood, still tacked for the day. He tightened the saddle cinch. "I'm going to check the herd before nightfall. I'll be back by the time you two are done."

"Sounds good." Colt and Jace waved as Dylan rode out of the barn.

Once Jace groomed Bingo and tacked him up, Colt showed him how to lead his horse to the arena. He taught his son a few groundwork basics and then helped him mount up. "We'll keep it at a walk today. Let you get used to how it feels to have a horse under you." After teaching the basics of walk on, whoa, and reining, Colt left Jace to practice while he tacked up Caitlyn's horse, Whiskey.

Together, they left the arena and rode along the trail

that led out to the pastures. Jace pointed at an old leaf-bare cottonwood tree. "Look! There's a swing."

"Yep, I remember swinging from that tree all summer long when I was your age."

"You did? Can I swing on it too?"

Colt chuckled. "Sure, but maybe we should wait for a warmer day."

"What's that cross there for? The one next to the tree. Is that somebody's grave?" Innocent hazel eyes peered up at him.

"That's a dog's grave. Caitlyn and Dylan's brother, Logan, had a K9 when he was in the Army. His name was Lobo. He was killed in an explosion in Afghanistan and the cross is here as a memorial."

"Man. That's sad."

"Yeah. It took Logan a long time to move past Lobo's death." Jace fell silent as they rode by the tree. "We'll ride to the edge of the woods and then turn around. I'm getting ready for some hot cocoa. How about you?"

"Me too!" His somberness forgotten, Jace bumped Bingo with his legs. The kind old horse picked up a gentle trot and Colt was about to tell Jace to ask him to walk, but when he saw his son's smile and his innate balance, he and Whiskey trotted along behind them.

Once they got back to the barn, Colt showed Jace how to put his tack away and brush his horse out again. "This is a nice way to thank your horse for taking you along on his back."

Dylan returned and did the same with Sampson. He stood next to Colt and while they watched Jace brush

Bingo's winter coat, he murmured. "I lost three head today."

Colt turned to face him. "Really? From the cold?"

"I doubt it. It's cold, but not enough to kill the cattle."

"What do you think happened, then? A bear, maybe?"

Dylan scratched his bearded chin. "I don't think so. There wasn't any sign of attack. No tracks, no blood. I'm not really sure what happened. I found them laying down by the creek."

"You know Adams lost a couple head this week, and Harbor did too. Are they getting into something, you think?"

"Probably, but I can't imagine what. I called Doc Moore. He's coming out in the morning to take a look. He had some other calls this afternoon, and I told him there was no rush. The carcasses will be frozen by morning."

11

—————

Dirk started the car's engine for what must have been the hundredth time since they began their turn watching Anthony Trova's Long Island estate. He cranked the heater. It was f-ing cold, and he was getting too old for this shit. He rubbed the top of his thighs up and down to create some warmth. Stakeouts were one thing. He was used to the bad food, worse coffee, and no sleep. Watching and waiting were a large part of his job as a Deputy US Marshal. But add freezing temperatures to the normal discomfort and it plunged him into a rotten mood.

Brad Something-or-other, his NYPD partner-for-the-day, groaned and shifted in his seat. He held his fingers in front of the heater vent. "There's been no movement all night after the lights went out at 11:30pm. When does our replacement team get here?"

"About an hour." Sterling unscrewed the top of his thermos and tilted the cylinder to pour. Three drops of coffee plopped into the plastic cup. "Come on!"

"Mine's gone too. Drank the last dregs at two this morning."

"Well, I'm not sitting out here any longer. Trova isn't here and his family hasn't even peeked outside." Sterling shifted the car into drive and turned up the long, paved road that led to the massive English-style, manor home in the countryside of Bridgehampton. "Someone inside has to know something."

"Sure, they do, but what makes you think they're going to share that information with you?" The cop chuffed.

"We won't know if we don't ask." Sterling parked at the bottom of elegant marble steps leading up to a set of impressive, black-enameled front doors. Ornate, twin brass-knockers glinted in the morning sun. Someone kept the lions' heads polished to a high sheen. "Let's go." Dirk led the way up the stairs and pounded the entrance with one of the golden levers.

It took five long minutes before the huge door swung silently inward, revealing a middle-aged woman dressed in the traditional black dress and white apron of a house-maid. She wore her dark hair pulled back into a sleek bun at the back of her head. "Good morning," she spoke in heavily accented English.

Dirk flashed his silver badge and ID. "I'm Deputy Marshal Sterling with the US Marshals Service." After the woman studied his badge, her gaze slid to the detective at his side. Jerking with a sudden awareness that they expected him to say something, Brad gave his name and fumbled for his NYPD credentials.

"How may I help you, gentlemen?" Her haughty expression displayed no desire to assist them.

Dirk answered, "We're looking for Anthony Trova. This is his residence, isn't it?"

"Yes, it is."

"May we see him?"

"No. Unfortunately, Mr. Trova sees no one without an appointment."

"Does a warrant for his arrest qualify as an appointment?" Dirk edged the toe of his boot inside the doorjamb. "Is he here?"

The housekeeper didn't so much as flinch at his mention of a warrant. "I'm sorry, Mr. Trova is not home at the moment. You'll have to come back another time."

"How about his wife? Or his children? Are they here?"

"I'm sorry, Deputy Sterling, none of the family is in residence at this time. They're in the city for the holidays." She was lying, but Dirk went along.

"Mr. Trova is in Manhattan with them?"

She drew in a steady breath. "Mr. Trova does not inform me of his personal plans. I'm sorry I could not be more helpful." The woman moved to close the door, but Dirk's boot blocked the way.

"Are you telling me you haven't heard from Mr. Trova since before Christmas? Be careful now, it's illegal to lie to an officer of the law." Something flickered in her dark eyes. He leaned in. "And, I'd hate to have to call Immigration to join us for this inquiry."

Her chin shot up defiantly, but concern filled her face. "I didn't say I hadn't heard from him, only that he doesn't share his schedule with me."

"Okay, then. Where is he?" Dirk pressed against the door opening it wider.

The woman stepped backward, crossing her arms. She glanced down a long hallway to her right and lowered her voice. "Mr. Trova was here two days ago. He came to pick up a food order from the chef for his driving trip. I don't expect him home for weeks." She placed her hand firmly on the door and pushed it against Dirk's boot. "Now, if you'll excuse me, I have work to do."

"Where did he go on his *driving trip?*"

"I don't know that information. As I said, the master of the house doesn't confide in me." She pressed the door harder.

"You have no ideas? No guesses?"

She sighed and sent another worried glance down the corridor. "He mentioned something about water. Perhaps Niagara Falls? I truly do not know. Now, good day, gentlemen." She shoved the door with both hands, and Dirk moved his foot. The great door slammed shut.

"Niagara Falls? This time of year?" Dirk descended the steps. "That doesn't seem likely."

"It's actually beautiful up there in the winter. Parts of the falls freeze, and the surrounding trees are coated in ice." Brad followed Dirk to the car. "It's awesome when they light it up at night. My wife says it's magical." The officer held up his hands and wiggled his fingers in the air laughing at his wife's description.

Dirk slid into the driver's seat. "So, Trova could be headed to Niagara Falls to see the magic… or to Florida to lay in the sun on the beach. Basically, we've got nothing." He slammed his hand against the steering wheel. "Let's do another search on all RVs purchased in the past six months. Look for Trova's name and all of his known busi-

nesses. And find out if the Manhattan team has discovered anything yet. Have they interviewed the family?" He
started the engine and drove away from the elegant estate.
"One thing is damn sure, I'm not going to sit around New
York anymore, hoping Trova will turn up."

12

On her way to the barn in the pre-dawn hours, Caitlyn checked the messages on her phone. There was a text from Colt she needed to respond to, but it would have to wait until she had time to call him. They had some serious issues they needed to work through, and texting wasn't going to cut it. She and Renegade entered the stall aisle. Danny was already feeding, and she watched him for several minutes. Something strange was going on with him. Something he felt the need to lie about, and she wanted to know what it was.

He turned to scoop grain and noticed her standing there. "Oh hey, Caitlyn. You about ready?"

"Yeah." She bent to stroke Renegade's head. "But are you sure it's okay to bring my dog to the racetrack?"

"Of course. He's well behaved. Dogs and horses go together. You'll see a lot of dogs there."

"Good. I don't want to stand out."

Together they loaded the horse trailer with all the supplies and feed they'd need during the day. They wrapped Triton's legs and blanketed him for the ride to the track, and they left the farm well before the sun made its morning appearance.

Danny pulled into the racing grounds and stopped at the guard shack next to the stable yard entrance. "Good morning. I'm Danny Franco, here with Triton from Pegasus."

A craggy older man bundled against the early chill checked Danny's name off on his list and pointed toward the barn. "You're in stall eleven."

Danny waved his thanks and parked the truck and trailer in a pull-through slot next to another rig and turned off the engine. "Here we are. This is our big chance."

"It's exciting. This reminds me of going to horse shows as a kid. Getting to the fairgrounds early and setting up camp."

They climbed down from the cab. Caitlyn backed Triton out of the trailer while Danny pulled the rolling tack chest from the truck's bed. Together, they made their way inside the stable row and found their designated spot. Other teams worked to settle their horses, and an excitement coursed through the early morning race community. Dogs sniffed each other in greeting while folks tossed jokes back and forth as easily as they shared coffee, and no one looked twice at her K9.

Caitlyn turned Triton into his stall and removed his lead rope while Danny opened the chest and pulled out two folding chairs. He hung his Pegasus racing silks and cap outside Triton's box and sat down to have some coffee. "Want a cup?" Caitlyn gratefully accepted the hot drink from Danny's thermos and sat next to him to watch the business in the barn. "You should go inside and check it out. Place a bet if you want to."

"I think I will," she blew across the surface of her coffee. "I grew up with horses, but I've never been to a racetrack. This sport is all new to me." She stood. "Do you need me to bring you anything?"

"No, I'm all set. My wife packed me some muffins. Want one for breakfast?"

Caitlyn gave him a half-smile. "I'm surprised you're eating. Don't jockeys starve themselves before a race?"

Danny pursed his lips. "Not this jockey." He unwrapped a nut-filled muffin and took a huge bite.

"Okay. We'll be back in a little while." Caitlyn strolled down the stable row with Renegade in tow, admiring the gorgeous racers. The racehorses were all tall and sleek. Every muscle in their graceful bodies was cut and well defined. Most wore blankets or sheets emblazoned with the logos of their home barns draped over their shaved coats.

Caitlyn wandered out across the staging area that would soon fill with the horses slated in the first race of the day. She crossed over to the spectator stands with the betting counters below. Climbing the stairs, she took in the empty racetrack with its freshly groomed footing, and a thrill zipped through her that had nothing to do with her investigation, and everything to do with being a part of the racing world. Smiling to herself, Caitlyn said, "Come on Ren. Let's go place a bet."

Triton's race was at two o'clock, and Caitlyn watched several of the morning's races before she reminded herself that she was here for a reason beyond horses. She and Renegade went back to the stables and walked slowly up one side and down the other listening for any chatter about the stolen horses. They passed a stall whose occupant must have been out racing. The space was empty except for a chair and locked tack chest. Renegade sniffed at the chest and then he smelled the seat. Caitlyn waited, but Renegade moved on.

The snippets of conversation centered mostly on the day's races and the various competitors. She was getting nowhere. Before long, it was time to get Triton ready for his race. Danny changed into his silks and carried his saddle to the jockey's locker room for his official weigh-in. When he returned, he and Caitlyn left Renegade at the stall and took Triton to the staging ring. She boosted Danny up to the saddle where he slid his toes into stirrups so short his knees rubbed against Triton's withers. Danny told her to lead Triton to the number six spot where they waited for the remaining sections to fill. A photographer took official race photos before the horses and their riders were announced and paraded in front of the cheering crowd.

Caitlyn passed the lead rope off to a rider and lead pony that guided Triton and Danny past the spectators to their gate. She darted up to the stands to watch Triton run. An announcer called out the race and fired the starter gun. The gates flew open, and they were off! Triton bolted from the number six slot. As the jockeys found their positions, Triton rounded the first bend in fourth place. "Go Triton!" Caitlyn yelled as she bounced on the balls of her feet.

Danny held his horse steady as they raced into the backstretch, but he released him on the final turn and Triton ignited. His stride lengthened as he stretched his nose forward. Danny encouraged him with his whip, and Triton soared. Caitlyn held her breath as the band of thundering hooves clamored toward the finish line. Triton came in second by a nose. So close!

As soon as the race was over Caitlyn sprinted to the stables, so she'd be there when Danny returned. When she got there, Renegade was gone. She looked up and down the alleyway and saw him pawing at the ground in front of the stall he had sniffed at earlier. She jogged over to him. "What is it, Ren? What did you find?"

Before she had a chance to see what her dog was digging at, Danny called to her from the end of the alley. "We did it, Caitlyn! This race was a qualifier for Panama Downs next week!"

She wasn't sure what they had done. After all, Triton had come in second and Caitlyn lost the money she'd bet on him. But she was happy that Triton did so well in his first official race.

"As soon as we rub Triton down, I'm going to collect my winnings." Danny turned the big horse into his stall and grabbed a towel to rub down his muscles and legs.

"What winnings? I thought you came in second."

"We did, but the bet was for Triton to place." Danny laughed and kissed Triton's muzzle.

"Isn't it illegal for you to bet on your own race?"

"Yes, but Triton's trainer placed the bet. He's just sharing a percentage with me."

Caitlyn thought that sounded unethical and went

against the intention of the rule but kept the thought to herself. "I lost my money. I bet on him to win." Caitlyn scrunched her brows together. "Maybe you need to teach me how to bet."

"For sure! When you bet on a horse to place, it's a bet that he'll either win or come in second. It doesn't pay as much as a win wager, but you have two chances to cash in instead of just one." He changed his damp towel out for a clean, dry one. "The most common types of bets are the win, place, and show bets. You placed a win bet. I bet on Triton placing. A show bet pays if your horse comes in first, second, or third. But you should try an exotic wager."

Caitlyn raised her eyebrows. "Exotic betting? Is that betting in the nude?" she teased.

Danny grinned. "No, it's when you bet on more than one horse. Those bets are more complicated, but you can win big for a small bet stake. There are the Quinella, Exacta, and Trifecta bets."

"I've heard of a trifecta, but not the other two. How do they work?"

"In the Quinella, you bet on two horses to come in first and second in any order. For the Exacta, you bet on two horses to come in first and second, only they have to come in the exact order you bet on to win."

"I'm guessing the Trifecta is the same, only with three horses?"

Danny gave her a thumbs up. "Exactly. You've got it."

Caitlyn bit her lip. "That sounds impossible."

"It's a game of chance. Of course, if you want, you can always box your bet. That means you still win no matter what order they come in if the three horses you pick come in first, second, and third."

"So, how much money did you win?"

"Two hundred bucks. Thank you very much."

At her side, a soft growl rumbled in Renegade's throat and drew Caitlyn's attention. Her nerves zinged in response, and she looked to see what he'd fixated on. He stared at the stall where he'd been pawing around earlier. A horse occupied the space now, and a young jockey sat on a tack chest near the opening. "What is it, Ren?" She stroked the top of his head. "Hey Danny, I'll be right back. I want to check something out." Danny nodded, and she and Renegade walked toward the stall in question.

Caitlyn said hello to the jockey, but Renegade ignored him, so she kept walking. A man ran up behind them, and Caitlyn's pulse lurched. Hot prickles shot across her neck, and she reached for her weapon, but the runner passed by them on their right. Her breath caught in her throat, and she chided herself for overreacting—again. She had to get a grip on herself. And yet, there was something about the man who ran past. He seemed familiar, though she couldn't place him.

Suddenly she knew. He was the man she'd seen yelling at Danny from the truck at the farm. Who was he? She called to Renegade, and they rushed back to Triton's stall. Danny wasn't there. "Danny?" she called. She asked the people sitting in front of the stall next to theirs if they'd seen him, but they shrugged and shook their heads. "Danny," she called again.

Renegade barked at her from a darkened stall several slots down. She ran to him and stifled a gasp. Danny lay crumpled in a heap on the ground, blood oozing from a small cut on his head. Caitlyn knelt next to him and gently shook his shoulder. "Danny?" He groaned and opened his eyes. Confusion filled his face as he stared at her. "Are you okay? Who did this to you?"

His eyes cleared, and he touched the cut on his head. Looking at the blood on his fingers, he said, "It's nothing." He pushed himself to his feet where he wavered for a second gaining his balance. "Let's get Triton loaded up and back to Pegasus."

"Danny, what's going on? I saw the man who was at the farm yesterday. Did he do this to you?" She pulled out her phone. "I'm calling 911."

"No!" Danny grabbed her arm. "Don't worry about it, Caitlyn. I'm fine and this has nothing to do with you. It's not your business." He stalked past her and tossed his things into the tack trunk. After buckling Triton's travel blanket and securing his leg pads, Danny thrust the lead rope at Caitlyn. "You load him up. I'll get everything else."

She waited until they were on their way home before she said, "I want you to tell me what happened to you today. I can help you. You ought to press assault charges."

"Stay out of it, Caitlyn. Please."

13

Colt was late to the office, and the phone was ringing as he came through the door. He'd stopped off at the café for a cinnamon roll and a cup of coffee to go, and he set his breakfast next to the keyboard on his desk. He picked up the receiver. "Sheriff Branson, here. How can I help you?" Propping the handset between his ear and shoulder he shrugged out of his coat and tossed it on one of the two chairs in front of his desk.

"Sheriff, it's Doctor Moore here. I'm calling from Reed Ranch. I'm out here checking on the three dead cows Dylan found down by the river on their land yesterday."

"Yeah, I was out there last night. What do you think is killing the local cattle, Doc? That's eight this week so far."

"I'm not entirely sure, yet. I've sent tissue and blood samples into the lab. I'll let you know what I find out."

"Is there another reason you're calling me about this, Doctor? Do you believe there was foul play?"

The veterinarian paused. "I don't know yet, but I think it's wise to keep you in the loop just in case."

"I appreciate that. It's strange to be sure. The affected ranches don't share property lines. Harbor's place is clear on the other side of town. It makes you wonder how on earth these dead cows could be connected."

"They might not be. It could be some odd coincidence."

"Sure... if you believe in coincidences." Which Colt did not. "I'll drive out and talk with the ranchers who've lost cattle again today and look for anything all the ranches have in common. I'll stop in at the feed store too. Jim might be able to shed some light on the situation. In fact, I'm sure he's hearing even more about this than we are." Jim Miller, owner of the local feed and tack store, knew all the ranchers in the area—and all their business.

"Sounds good," Doctor Moore replied. "Please call me if you learn anything. If there is some type of contagion, we'll need to stop the spread as fast as possible. We might end up quarantining the affected herds."

"Will do." Colt hung up the phone and reached for his coat and breakfast. He jogged out to his Jeep. Forty minutes later, he arrived at Greg Harbor's ranch. The old rancher snickered when Colt asked if he'd recently grained his herd or if he'd put out any new mineral licks. "How do you think cows survived for thousands of years before feed stores existed? I never give my herd any of that money-burning nonsense."

Next, Colt drove out to the Adams' place and asked the same questions. "Yes, sir. I've been supplementing the hay with a mix of corn, oats, and barley. I get it in bulk over at the feed store."

Colt jotted down the various additional feeds on a small notebook he kept in his breast pocket. "Any mineral licks or such?"

"Yeah, I throw several mineral blocks out there, and I keep a hundred-pound molasses lick out in the pasture too. I like to give them a little boost, especially in the cold months."

"You get those over at the feed store, too?"

"Of course." The wiry rancher crossed his arms. "You think we got ahold of bad feed or something?"

"I don't know, but I'll call you right away when I find out."

"Thanks, Sheriff."

On his way back through Moose Creek, Colt stopped in at the feed store. "Hey, Jim. How's business treating you?"

The tall, lanky shop owner brushed off the counter with his large hand. "Pretty good. How's the law serving you?" Jim had owned the feed store for over ten years. He bought his father-in-law out shortly after Jim and his wife got married.

"Not too bad this year. So far, it's been nice and quiet."

"Well, that's a good thing in your line of work I suspect. 'Course, it's only one week into the new year, so far."

"Indeed," Colt chuckled, but he wasn't sure he agreed that quiet was a good thing. It wasn't like he wanted his life to be at risk all the time, but he'd like a little more excitement than coaxing kittens out of trees and prodding dead cows. "Listen, Jim. I'm wondering if you can help me figure something out. In the past several days, I've had reports of three ranches with cattle dying suddenly. Have you heard anything about this going on?"

"Well, I knew about the Adams' cows. Who else has lost cattle?"

"Old Harbor and also Dylan Reed."

Jim chuckled. "Harbor wouldn't darken my doorstep. He likes to ranch the old-fashioned way." Jim used air-quotes when he said it. "Whatever that means. I'm sorry to hear about Dylan though. He's had a rough couple of years."

"He's doing better, but *nobody* can afford to lose cows."

"No, sir. That's a fact. What do you think is causing it?" Jim stuck his thumbs in his belt loops and rocked back on his heels.

Colt leaned his elbow on the counter. "Well, honestly, I figured maybe some bad feed came through or something was wrong with the cow licks. That would make the most sense except for the fact that Harbor doesn't give his cattle either of those things."

"I'd sure hate to think something I sold was making their herds sick." Jim looked stricken by the thought.

"It wouldn't be your fault, Jim. But we'd need to pull it from your inventory if that were the case."

"Absolutely. Do you think I should do that anyway, just to be safe?"

"Have any other ranchers complained about sick cattle?"

Jim reached under the counter and pulled out a well-worn three-ring binder. Inside it he kept a phone log, and he leafed through the pages. He paused, tapping his finger on one entry. "Henderson called two weeks ago saying that one of his cows had bloat... but I think she was okay after he stuck a stomach tube down her throat." He flipped through several more pages. "I don't see anything else that seems connected."

"Do you have any record of who has purchased feed and molasses licks over the past couple of months? If we find out there is something in one of them that's killing cattle, we'll want to notify anyone who has bought some."

"I'll try to put a list together. I'll pull those licks from the shelves for now. The grain, too. Just in case."

"It's probably a good idea, at least until we figure out what's happening. Thanks, Jim. Say hello to the family."

Rather than drive all the way out to Reed Ranch, Colt called Dylan, but he didn't answer. He hardly ever did during the day because there was no cell coverage out on the range. Colt left a message filling Dylan in on the little he knew about the cows that had died around Moose Creek.

When Colt got back to the office, his phone buzzed. It was Allison. "Hey, what's up?"

"I've been online searching for apartments or houses to rent from Spearfish to Gillette and everywhere in between. First of all, there are hardly any places decent enough for me and Jace to live in, and the few that are, we simply can't afford. But secondly, I've also been checking out some places in Missouri. Did you know that housing is almost ten percent lower there than in Wyoming? Not to mention there are so many more opportunities for Jace in a city."

"Allison, you and I both turned out just fine growing up in the country."

"Colt, hear me out." She paused long enough to make him uncomfortable. "Would you consider moving to Missouri? Jace has friends there... and so do I. You could get a job as a cop."

"And what about Catie? She's a part of this too, remember?"

"Caitlyn has a federal job. She could probably work anywhere. Will you think about it? I don't know what else to do. We can't keep sponging off my parents."

"Didn't you agree to take over your dad's tire business? What will he do if you move away?"

"I'm sure he could find someone else. I've got things in order there and now it's boring. I need more excitement in my life."

"So, this is all about you?"

"And Jace. Stop being so selfish, Colt. Not everyone is suited to living a lonely rural life."

Colt pinched the bridge of his nose. "I'll help you find a place, Allison. Just give me a little more time."

"Until then, do you think you could forward me some cash?"

"I pay you a healthy amount of child support already. What do you need cash for?"

"You're not my husband, so I don't have to tell you that."

"That's true, and I don't have to loan it to you either." Colt leaned back in his chair and closed his eyes. He tried not to let her push his buttons, but she was too good at it.

"Fine. I need some new clothes... and so does Jace. I

barely make enough money to buy groceries, let alone anything extra."

Colt had noticed Jace's winter coat was getting too small. "How much do you need?"

"A thousand should do."

He sat straight up. "A thousand dollars? You've got to be kidding me. I don't have an extra thousand dollars lying around." Caitlyn did, but that was *her* money, and he wasn't about to ask her for any of it. "Listen, I'll try to get whatever Jace needs, but you're on your own. Why don't you ask your dad for a loan?"

"That's fine, Colt," Allison snapped. "But just so you know, if I lived in Missouri, I could afford new clothes *and* I'd have a place to wear them."

14

William Hayes. Today was the last time he'd be using that name, Bill thought as he shuffled into the windowless interview room in the USMS building in Nashville. His doctors had released him from the hospital, but he was still in a ton of pain from the gunshot wound in his thigh. His leg would never be the same after losing a chunk of muscle from his quadriceps. The surrounding skin that was peppered with buckshot was magenta, puckered, and sore. Hot spasms of agony shot up his leg, making his eyes water.

A lady cop pulled two chairs out from the table, one for him to sit on and the other for his foot. He eased onto the seat, grateful to prop his injured leg up and rest. He folded his hands on the tabletop and waited for the questions to start. Five more people filed into the room. The two uniformed cops stood guard by the door. His attorney took the chair next to him, and together they faced three US Marshals across the table.

The one marshal wearing a suit began the interview.

"I'm Nashville Chief Deputy Marshal Cook, and these are US Deputy Marshals Collins and Rodgers. We're here to take your statement and guard you until you testify against Charles Rutledge. After that, we'll give you a new identity and location—a new life. We'll keep you safe as long as you provide us with useful information in the prosecution of Rutledge and the drug and arms dealers you worked with."

Bill's chest constricted. He wanted to believe the US Marshals could hide him, but he knew better. Hiding might prolong his life for a few months—even a year—but he'd never really be rid of the cartel members he'd shot at. They wanted their drugs, or the money, and they had neither. He had killed one of their buddies and they'd want revenge. Those kinds of guys took what you owed them out of your hide and out of the skin of those you loved. Thankfully, he didn't have any loved ones. But since he also didn't have the funding to skip the country and disappear like his boss did, his only hope lay with the three marshals staring at him. He'd have to rely on what was most likely empty promises from the witness protection program.

Deputy Rogers shoved a pad of paper and a pen at him before turning on a recorder. "Tell us everything you know about Charles Rutledge, his wife Tansey, and their business. Do you know where he is? How long were you involved in his drug trafficking schemes?"

Bill pushed the pad back toward the marshal's side of the table. "How can I be sure you're gonna be able to protect me? What guarantees do *I* have?"

Deputy Collins clasped her hands together on the

table and leaned forward. "WITSEC has never lost anyone who followed the rules of the program. So, I guess you can be sure of your safety to the same degree you're willing to do as you're told."

Bill pulled the legal pad back and picked up the pen. "I'll write everything I know about the drugs and guns, but I don't know for sure where Rutledge is. It's not like we was drinking buddies or nothing."

Chief Deputy Cook smoothed his fingers along the edge of the table and pushed himself to his feet. "Just write down what you remember. Anything you can think of. Did Rutledge ever talk about going on trips abroad? Or did he mention people he knew who lived in other countries?"

Bill met Cook's gaze. "There was one guy who came to the farm for a couple of weeks last summer. He was foreign. Had some kind of accent." Bill rolled the pen between his thumb and fingers while he gathered his thoughts.

"Good." Cook lifted his suit coat from the back of his chair. He pushed his arms into the sleeves and shrugged on the gray jacket. "Write it all down. Tell us how many dealers there were and what they looked like. Do you remember hearing any names? What did the foreign visitor's accent sound like? Did he say anything about his home or the general area he came from?"

Of the three marshals, Bill liked the Chief best. He was helpful and treated Bill with kindness. In fact, Cook's questions helped him remember things he hadn't thought of. "Yeah, now that you mention it. The man sounded kinda Mexican, I think. They talked about going to see some hippos or something like that."

Collins tilted her head. "Like at the zoo? Do you think they were setting up a meet at the zoo, or what?"

"No… hippo dome, maybe. And some other word like Camaro. That's it—the Hippo Camaro."

Rogers tossed his head back and dropped his pen on the table. "Hippo Camaro? Seriously? What the hell is that?"

Collins chuckled. "Do you mean, the Hipódromo Camarero?" Collins jotted the name on a pad of paper.

"Maybe. I don't know. I'm just telling you what I heard. I also remember Mrs. Rutledge saying something about not liking to fly over the water. She was always cry-babying about something."

Cook opened the interview room door. "That's good, Mr. Hayes. Just get it all down on paper." He addressed the remaining marshals. "I'm headed out to the farm. Meet me out there when you're finished here."

"Chief," Bill sat up abruptly, causing a stab of white heat in his thigh. He sucked in a breath. "Where are you going to send me after I testify? Do I get any say?" Bill hoped it was somewhere warm. A southern boy, born and bred, he hated cold and snow. "Maybe it could be some-where tropical?"

"No, you don't get any say, unfortunately. And we won't discuss your future destination until after the trial is over." The chief gave him a nod and left the room. All other eyes turned back to Bill.

Collins slapped the table startling him. "It won't be at

an all-inclusive resort, you know. This isn't a vacation. Now, get to work, Hayes. We don't have all day."

Bill sat back in his chair and hooked one arm over the back. "I think I'll hold out until you tell me where I'm going. I'll keep the info to myself until we agree on a final destination."

Collins's chair scraped angrily across the floor as she rose to her feet. "Not a problem. We'll just dump you out on the street. How long do you think you're gonna survive out there? Soon as word gets out that you're out of protective custody at the hospital, how long before the drug dealers show up? An hour? Two? You'd be extremely lucky to make it until nightfall."

"If you do that, I won't live to testify." Bill tried to sound cocky, but even he could hear the fear in his voice.

"That's my point, numb nuts." Collins glared at him, shaking her head.

His threat hadn't given him the leverage he'd hoped for. "But you need my testimony. You don't have any evidence without me."

"We'll get the evidence we need somewhere else. And we'll find Rutledge without you too; it'll just take a little longer." The deputy marshal tapped her partner on his shoulder. "Come on. Let's get out of here." Rogers nodded, stacked his papers, and closed them in a file folder.

"Wait!" Bill stretched out his hand as if he could stop them from leaving. "I'll write it down. Don't be so sensitive. We have a deal." He lifted the pen and started scribbling down all he could remember about Charles Rutledge's business. "Oh, and I just remembered. That guy I told you about... he wasn't from Mexico."

DIRK AND BRAD had been driving for over two hours on their way back to Manhattan from Bridgehampton, and still they were only on the outskirts of Queens. "I hate the traffic in this city." Dirk glanced at the man sitting next to him tapping on his phone screen. "What are you looking at?"

"We just got the warrant to search Trova's Long Island residence and his apartment in Manhattan." The New York cop peered at him from the corner of his eye. "What do you want to do?"

"Right on time." Dirk rolled his eyes and released a puff of frustration. Gripping the steering wheel hard, he said, "Well, I'm sure as hell not turning around and going back out to Trova's estate. Besides, NYPD and the FBI can handle searching for evidence. Trova's not at either location, and he's the one we're after. I'm not concerned with his family. Even if we find them, they won't tell us anything." The taillights on the sedan in front of him flashed red and Dirk slammed on the brakes. His tires squealed on the pavement in his narrow escape from a rear-end collision.

Hank braced his feet on the floor as he flew forward against his seat belt. He sent Dirk a wry glance but with his New York attitude, he continued as though they hadn't almost crashed into another car. "There could be information in either location about the RV we're looking for, though."

"Could be." The last thing Dirk wanted was to be tied

up with a band of investigators methodically going through every receipt and scrap of paper in the houses.

"Do you want in on the search?" Brad cleared his throat. "If not, you can drop me off at Trova's penthouse. I'll hunt for any vehicle records he might have there."

"Yeah, okay." Dirk pushed the air recycle button on the dash. "These exhaust fumes are killing me."

"Welcome to New York."

Dirk missed the fresh air of Montana. Not to mention the traffic-free highways. "I'll drop you and then go to the office to see what I can find out about Trova's business and any known shell corporations. He probably bought the RV with false identification and a false bank account."

"Hopefully one of us will find something useful. I'll contact the search team in Bridgehampton and let them know what we're looking for, though I doubt he keeps his paperwork lying around the house."

Dirk agreed. "It's more likely kept at his attorney's office." His phone vibrated in his back pocket, and he tilted his hip so he could reach it.

The call came from an NYPD admin. "I'm glad I got ahold of you, sir. I just took a message from a Sergeant Depew with South Carolina State Patrol. He reported seeing a luxury RV with two older men inside at a rest stop on southbound I-95 near the Georgia border."

"Did he get a plate number?" Dirk's system revved. Finally, they might have a lead. He ignored the condescending voice at the back of his mind murmuring that there were hundreds of RVs driven by two old geezers out on the road. "How about a description of the men? Was anyone else with them? Any dogs?"

The admin hesitated. "He got a license plate number from New York. I'm texting it to you now. I don't know about the dog, though. I'll ask. Or do you want me to patch you through to him?"

"No need but have him put out a BOLO for the RV, and I need you to run the plates. Let me know what you find." Dirk ended the call and told Brad what was going on.

Traffic was heavy on the Queensboro Bridge and Dirk tapped his fingers on the steering wheel trying to release his agitation. Suddenly, he jerked the wheel and zoomed into the next lane. The driver of the moving van he cut off lay on his horn.

Brad gripped the handle on his door. "Good job. You have to be aggressive to drive in this city. People expect it."

"If you say so."

Dirk's phone buzzed again. "I ran the plates, like you asked," the admin's voice took on a conspiratorial tone. "Sure enough, the RV was purchased through a company called T&T Holdings, LLC. I Googled the name, and the company has a one-page website that doesn't lead anywhere. A deeper search informed me that T&T Holdings, LLC is a New York based company but has no employees."

Dirk chuffed. "No surprise there." The name T&T sounded right up Trova's ego-centric alley. "I'm dropping the cop who's with me off at Trova's apartment building and then I'm driving to the airport. Will you please find Deputy Marshal Flannigan, tell him about T&T Holdings, and give him an office where he can do more research on the company?"

"Of course."

"Thanks. And get me listed on the next flight to Savannah." Dirk clicked off and then explained his change in plans to Brad. "The fact that the RV in Savannah has New York plates and was also purchased by a shell company in New York is cause enough for me to go down there and check it out. Keep me posted on your search from this end."

After dropping Brad off, Dirk turned toward LaGuardia International Airport. On his way, he called the USMS office in Savannah and spoke with one of their deputies. "I need you to send a team to apprehend an RV currently in South Carolina, headed southbound on I-95. The vehicle is being tailed by a South Carolina State Patrol Officer. It's likely the RV driver will cross the state line and stop somewhere near Savannah for the night." Dirk gave them the license plate number. "Use caution. The occupants might be older, but they know how to handle themselves and they're more than likely armed."

"I'll organize it right away."

"Thanks. And could you reserve me a rental car? I'll be on the flight coming in from La Guardia later tonight."

15

Caitlyn and Danny fed the horses their evening rations in silence. After tacking his second-place ribbon to Triton's stall door, Danny left for home. Caitlyn knelt next to Renegade, put her arm around his shoulders, and watched Danny drive away. He was hiding something. But what? Could he be involved with the horse theft somehow? Did he know more than he'd been saying about Rutledge? She'd be furious if she found out he'd been lying to her all along. "You suspect something too, don't you Ren? I wonder what you smelled at that stall?"

Frustrated, Caitlyn paced the length of the stable row and back. Her phone rang. One of the deputies up at the house was calling. "Yeah, Reed here."

"Chief Cook is here and is about to head home, but he wants to talk to you first."

"I'm on my way." She clicked off. "Come on, Ren. Our presence is requested."

The Chief Deputy stood before a blazing fire enjoying

a drink in the library when she entered. He had a distinguished air about him. He was tall and trim. Gray diffused his military-taper haircut. "Care to join me?" He gestured to a silver tray boasting a top-shelf single malt and a cut crystal tumbler.

"Don't mind if I do." She poured herself a healthy amount of the amber liquid and added two small, horseshoe-shaped ice cubes to chill her whiskey. Renegade found the perfect spot to nestle on the carpet in front of the fire and he laid down with a satisfied groan.

"How did the race go today?" Cook assessed her over the rim of his glass. Caitlyn was sure those steel-blue eyes missed nothing.

"Triton came in second by a nose. It was close."

"You sound disappointed."

Caitlyn gave him a self-deprecating grin. "Because I bet on him for the win." She sat in a wingback and watched the firelight ricochet through the amber liquid in her glass before sipping its buttery heat.

The chief beamed. "I bet on him to show. The payout isn't as much as it would have been for a place bet, but I still won a fair amount."

"Chief, I'm surprised at you." Caitlyn chuckled into her glass.

"Tell me, did you learn anything useful while you were at the track? Hear any stable gossip about the horse thieves?"

"No, but I found Danny unconscious and dumped into an empty stall this afternoon." She filled the chief in on the incident with the man in the truck the day before.

"Our jockey is keeping secrets, and I'm betting it's all connected somehow."

"Could be, but if Danny was part of the horse thievery, then he wouldn't need to work here for such a small wage."

"I suppose... unless he's using the job as a cover to keep tabs on things here."

Cook straightened his shirt sleeve by tugging the cuff. "When's the next race?"

"Day after tomorrow. Danny said that today's local race was a qualifier to race in Panama Downs in Florida." Caitlyn rested her head back against the leather chair.

"I sat in on the first few minutes of Collins's and Rogers's interview with our WITSEC witness." Cook finished his drink.

"Is he going to be any help?"

"It's hard to say." Cook's phone dinged, and he swiped the screen with his thumb. "It's Rogers. His text says Hayes thought he heard Rutledge's wife say she wanted to go to the Hipódromo Camarero. Collins recognized the name but couldn't place it. Seems they've looked up the name and surprise, surprise, it's a horse racing track in Puerto Rico."

"Looks like the mouse can't stay away from the cheese." Caitlyn sucked in a molded ice cube and stared at the fire while it melted on her tongue. "Can Danny keep racing? He's scheduled Triton to race several more times, and I know his family could really use the money. Especially since he's no longer on Rutledge's payroll."

"I suppose you can keep it up until we auction the

house off. Then we'll have to rely on more traditional tactics. What about the secrets he's keeping?"

"Spending time with him is the best way to find out what those are. How do you feel about the races down in Florida?" She bit down on her lip waiting for his reaction.

He shocked her with his calm response. "Will you be traveling down there with him?"

"Uh... I'd like to. But I'd need to hire another ranch hand to manage the barn while I'm gone."

"I suppose we could pay for that with the racing proceeds. Hire someone who knows what they're doing, and then they can train one of the marshals assigned to inventorying the house to help him as needed."

"Yes, sir. Thank you, sir." Caitlyn stood as he readied to leave.

"Keep me apprised." He slid his suit coat on. "I'm eager to track Rutledge down. Plus, I need to know when to place my next bet." He smirked and left the room.

Caitlyn returned to her chair and sipped the ridiculously smooth scotch. She'd never be happy with the cheap stuff again. That Rutledge character sure knew how to live. She imagined the southern gentleman hiding out in some palatial home in Puerto Rico. Caitlyn realized the house had gone quiet, and she suddenly felt lonely. Lifting her phone, she dialed Colt.

"It's so good to hear your voice. I'm sorry about last night." Caitlyn closed her eyes, and savoring another sip, she pictured her husband sitting by the fire in her... *their* cabin.

"Me too. I shouldn't bug you with my personal issues when you're on a job."

"Yes, you should. You should always bug me—with anything."

His laugh rolled through the phone and warmed her even more than the whiskey. Caitlyn filled Colt in on the horse racing case.

"So, you're going to Florida, now?"

"Just for a couple of days. With any luck, one of the stolen horses will either show up at a track, or someone will spill the beans about it. I know I'm grasping at straws, but that's all we have. The guy they're putting in WITSEC hasn't given us much to go on yet. He'd better cough something up soon, or he'll be out in the cold, on his own."

"I miss you."

"I miss you too. You could meet me in Panama City."

"I wish. But I've got the mysterious case of dying cattle I need to solve."

"Sounds fascinating." Caitlyn giggled. "Be careful. Cows kick, you know."

"Not when they're dead."

16

———

Triton came in first place in his final race in Tennessee before they all headed to Florida. Caitlyn and Danny were giddy. She had learned nothing of interest at the track and continued struggling to remember she was supposed to be on a case, not diving headlong into the world of horse-racing.

Danny honked the truck's horn in celebration as they pulled out of the parking lot and turned for home at the end of the day. "Can you be ready to leave by four o'clock tomorrow morning?"

"Absolutely. Early mornings aren't a problem for me. It's Renegade who likes to sleep in." Caitlyn giggled and stroked the beautiful silken head that rested in her lap. Her dog swiped her knuckles with his warm pink tongue.

"Right." Danny chuckled as he merged onto the highway.

Caitlyn watched the headlights of the car behind them from the side-view mirror. "How does your wife feel about you going on a road trip with a woman she doesn't know?"

"She's fine. She'd come too, but it's easier to stay home with the boys."

"I bet."

"And your husband? How does he feel about you being on a road trip with a man you just met? Or more importantly for that matter, about you being a federal marshal?"

"He's used to me working with men. He knows I can take care of myself." The terrifying image of a cloth saturated with chloroform covering her nose and mouth flashed across her mind, catching her off guard. A choking sound clogged her throat, and she stopped breathing. Thankfully, her brain took over, excusing the emotion, and commanded her lungs to draw in air. One, two, three, four. Hold, six, seven. And out, two, three, four, five.

"Are you okay? You sound like you're choking." Danny glanced at her with concern.

Renegade sat up and licked her cheeks. "I'm good." She buried her face in his shoulder and silently repeated her calming breath exercise two more times. Was she ever going to get fully past her horrific memories? Her fear?

It was a ten-hour drive to Panama City the next day, and Caitlyn and Danny took turns driving every couple of hours. They hauled two horses in the trailer to race on this trip. The air was brisk at lunchtime when they pulled into a rest stop and took the colts out of the trailer so they could stretch their legs. Danny cleaned manure from the trailer while Caitlyn fed and watered Triton and his half-brother, Neptune. While she and Danny ate sandwiches his wife had packed for them, Caitlyn tossed a bumper for Renegade to chase. He, more than anyone, needed to burn off his pent-up energy.

Once they arrived at the Panama Downs racetrack, they signed in and unloaded the horses. After getting them settled in their stalls, Danny set up two chairs on either side of a large cooler and the tack chest they would use as tables.

Caitlyn checked her watch. "We have enough time to go to the hotel and get a shower before dinner, if you want."

"Sounds good. We can come back here to eat. There are a couple of restaurants here, and it might be good to hang around and meet other race teams. See if we can learn anything. Maybe someone has heard something about our stolen horses."

"Perfect. I'd like to get the lay of the land before we go, though. Will you show me around?"

Danny gave her a quick tour of the Panama Downs stables, the pre-race staging area, and the stands. "Inside is much like the track back home, only fancier. There are betting windows, a couple of bars, some electronic slot machines and other wagering games, and some snack-type places to eat. The casino is upstairs next to Beaux Chevaux, the track's pricey upscale restaurant."

Caitlyn followed him through the crowded building. He pointed to the glass wall of an elegant restaurant upstairs. "We can eat there if we win."

"Why if we win?"

"Can't afford it, otherwise."

"Yes, we can. I'll expense it." She clapped her hand on

Danny's shoulder. "You want to find criminals? Follow the money."

Caitlyn had nothing nice enough to wear to Beaux Chevaux, though. It was the type of place that required men to don jackets. So, she and Danny stopped at a mall on their way to the hotel. She found a shimmery purple dress on sale, which made the price of the gold strappy sandals and matching clutch slightly more palatable, and Danny bought a sports coat at J. C. Penney's. Caitlyn convinced herself the expense was necessary since she decided to go undercover as a wealthy horse owner.

At the hotel, Caitlyn hurried through her shower. She dried her hair and left it loose, letting it curl naturally in long walnut waves. She applied mascara, a dust of blush, and a touch of pink lip gloss, nodding to herself in the mirror. It would do. Before she left, she made sure Renegade was comfortable in his portable kennel in the pet friendly hotel room. "I won't be late. You be a good boy. Okay?" She gave him a pile of toys and a Kong filled with dog treats, but still he looked sad when she closed the door. His amber eyes pulling at her heartstrings.

She met Danny in the lobby, and he whistled when he saw her. "Wow! You look pretty damn good when you wash the dirt off."

Caitlyn laughed and tugged at her dress. "Thanks. I hope I can pull this off. I'm much more comfortable in my cowboy boots."

When they entered Beaux Chevaux, the host led them toward a table in the back. On the way, Caitlyn told Danny she was going to stop at the bar to order a drink.

"It'll give me a chance to look around. Maybe I'll hear some gossip about our missing horses."

The drink counter in the lounge was an oval that mimicked the racetrack it overlooked. There were few empty spots along the gleaming mahogany bar, but she squeezed in and placed her order. Not knowing if Panama Downs had its own signature cocktail, she ordered a mint julep for the fun of it. When the bartender returned with her icy glass, she handed him her credit card, but he waved her off.

"It's already been taken care of."

"What do you mean?"

He tilted his head toward the end of the oval counter and Caitlyn's gaze followed his gesture. A darkly handsome man, she guessed to be in his early fifties, with silver sprinkling the black hair at his temples, raised his glass to her. A ghost of a smile crossed his mouth as he studied her with his almost-black eyes. Her natural reaction was to decline the drink, but then she remembered this was why she was there. She took in his half-carat, diamond pinky-ring and expensive silk suit and wondered what information she might learn from this man who was clearly comfortable on the opulent side of the track.

She raised her glass, smiled, and mouthed, "Thank you."

The well-dressed man turned and spoke to someone standing behind him before he made his way across the bar to her. When he approached, the people crowded next to her moved out of his path, making room for him. The man he'd spoken to looked vaguely familiar, but Caitlyn couldn't place him before her benefactor slid into position. Caitlyn opened her clutch, slipped her wedding ring off, and dropped it inside. She'd play to this guy's advances and see if she could learn the identity of the man with whom he had spoken.

"Good evening." His cultured voice held a slight European accent.

"Hello. Thank you for the drink."

"My pleasure. I'm Guillon Favre. I don't believe I've seen you here before. Certainly, I would have remembered if I had."

"No, you're right. This is my first time." Caitlyn held her hand out toward him. "I'm Caitlyn..." she scrambled for a cover name and went with the first one to cross her mind. She hoped it would work. "Rutledge."

Guillon's eyes shifted slightly, and she would have missed it if she wasn't watching him intently. He took her fingers in his manicured hand and pressed them gently. For a surreal second, she thought he was going to kiss the back of her hand in some old-world manner, but he stopped short with a gentle bow. "It is my honor to make your acquaintance. Tell me, are you a relative of the Rutledge's of Pegasus Farms?"

Panic fisted in Caitlyn's belly. Why had she picked *that* name? Rookie mistake. What if this man was friends with Charles and Tansey Rutledge? It was too late; she'd bet on the name and now she had to see it through. "A niece."

"Charming. I've done some business with your uncle." Guillon leaned against the bar. "Will he be joining you?"

"No. I'm here on my own, this time." Caitlyn let her gaze drop as though she were uncertain of herself. Maybe this guy knew something that could help them find

Rutledge. She'd play this charade out and gather what information she could.

"Are you here with horses? Or simply as a wagering spectator?"

Relieved to change the subject away from her false relationship to the Rutledge's, Caitlyn released a soft laugh. "Both. I brought horses and I'm certainly planning to wager. And you?"

"The same." He touched her elbow. "Please, Caitlyn, will you do me the honor of dining with me tonight?"

She glanced to the back of the restaurant. "I—"

"Ah, you're looking for the man you came in with." His dark eyes held a warm humor. "Your jockey, I presume?"

"Yes." He'd obviously watched her enter the restaurant... had he seen her before then? She was going to have to stay in character from now on. Especially if she wanted to find out who the man Guillon was speaking with at the bar. There was something about the unknown man that niggled at the edge of her mind. She was certain she'd seen him before.

"I've already arranged for his meal. I'm sure he'll understand."

"I see." She raised her brows. This man was awfully sure of himself.

His smile broadened. "You think this presumptuous of me."

"Yes, as a matter of fact." Guillon's smooth confidence was over the top, but it made her job a whole lot easier.

"Forgive me. I am accustomed to getting what I want. Sometimes I forget my manners. Of course, we could ask him to join us—if you prefer."

Wow, this guy was slick. Caitlyn had no doubt at all that Guillon Favre acquired whatever he pursued. She sought a glimpse of Danny once again and saw a server open a bottle of wine at his table and pour him a glass. Danny's eyes met hers. He smiled and raised his glass to her.

Guillon stood close enough that she breathed in his subtle spice cologne. His fingertips barely pressed the inside of her elbow, yet the touch bore a possessive quality as he quietly observed her interaction with Danny.

"It seems he's in good hands." Caitlyn offered him a smile. "Thank you. And I'd love to join you."

"Wonderful." Guillon's gaze shifted to the host who nodded in return. His eyes then darted to the man he'd left on the other side of the bar before they returned to her. "Come." He slid his smooth hand around her elbow and guided her to follow the host up a spiral staircase to a solitary table overlooking the track and the grounds beyond.

"What a beautiful view," she marveled.

"Indeed." Guillon's eyes flitted over her figure and his lips curved appreciatively. He held her chair for her before he sat. Immediately, the host poured two glasses of a full-bodied Cabernet—the best wine she'd ever tasted. She never saw her dinner date place an order, but within minutes an appetizer of crabmeat in a cream sauce dolloped inside delicate pastry cups appeared on their table, followed later by a perfectly grilled fillet mignon with tender asparagus Oscar and roasted garlic potatoes.

Both Guillon's conversation and manners were impeccable, and Caitlyn worked hard to match them. An artistic confection arrived for dessert, and it baffled Caitlyn how to get past the spun sugar decoration to taste the creamy chocolate goodness below.

Guillon chuckled. "It's impressive, but admittedly difficult to enjoy. Allow me." With a knife and fork, he gracefully lifted the golden sugared-lace and set it aside. He waited for her to sample the crème de chocolate and studied her while she savored it. "I've truly enjoyed your company this evening, Caitlyn. I hope you'll join me in my private box to watch the races tomorrow."

"That's so kind of you, but I'm sure you have other friends, or business acquaintances you need to spend time with. The man you left at the bar when you came to meet me, for example."

Guillon's eyes flickered before he said, "He won't be joining us. However, I do have some friends who will, and it will be my pleasure to introduce you to them. Which races are your horses in?"

Caitlyn didn't know, and she thought fast. "I'm not actually sure. I'm very new to the racing world and I'm relying on Danny, my jockey, to teach me the ropes."

"His assistance is no longer necessary. I will be happy to guide you." Guillon reached for her hand and lifted it. Turning her wrist, he kissed her palm in a manner that felt somehow more intimate than a kiss on the lips. Colt would punch Guillon's elegant mouth for taking such liberty with his wife. How was she ever going to explain this situation to her husband?

"Thank you for the offer, but I brought my dog with me. I'm sure they don't allow dogs in the stands, and I can't leave him alone all day."

"Your dog?" Humor filled his eyes. "Don't tell me you carry a Pomeranian in your purse?"

She laughed at the thought. "Hardly. My dog is a Belgian Malinois who would never lower his standards enough to be carried in a purse."

"If your dog is the only obstacle holding you back from spending your afternoon with me, then bring him along. There are no rules about dogs in my box."

"Really? You wouldn't mind? He's very well behaved."

"Then, by all means."

Caitlyn smiled, more to herself than at Guillon. Colt would feel better if he knew Renegade was with her. He was like having a hairy chaperone. One with very sharp teeth.

Later that night, when Caitlyn was in her room, curled up with Renegade on the hotel couch, she called Colt. When he didn't answer, she left a quick message telling him she missed him, then texted Dirk: **I saw a man tonight who I couldn't place, but I can't shake the feeling that I know him from somewhere. Do you have a photo of Anthony Trova?**

17

_____

Colt stared down at the massive black lumps lying still in the snow. Three more cattle, lost. "Have you changed any of their feed lately?" Colt asked Paul Quince, the most recent rancher to report dead cows. "Or did they get into anything unusual that you noticed?"

"Nope. They've been eating hay cut from my own fields, nothing new there. They have the same molasses licks I've given them for years. I dragged these carcasses up here and moved my herd out to the far pasture this morning just in case the troughs are contaminated with somethin'. I can't afford to lose anymore cattle."

"That's a wise idea. Did these cows look sick in the past few days? Any clue they weren't well?"

Paul crossed his arms over his chest. "I didn't see anything, but you know how it is, with a hundred head. I don't check each one closely every day."

Colt nodded and pulled the neck of his coat closed at his throat. It was three degrees out and a bitter wind whipped down into the valley from the mountains making it feel even colder.

"Let's get inside, Sheriff. No need to freeze our asses off out here trying to figure this out."

Colt gratefully accepted a hot mug of coffee, if for no other reason than to warm his icy fingers. The men stood near a wood-burning stove and discussed possible reasons cattle might be dying in the Moose Creek Valley.

Colt's phone dinged with an incoming text from Dylan: **Lost a yearling bull-calf this morning. His mama isn't looking good either. Found him frozen in the mud down by the creek. Dr. Moore told me to check in with you. Brought the cow up to the barn.**

"That message was from Dylan Reed. He just lost another calf, too."

"Well, I'll be damned, Sheriff. What's going on around here?"

Colt took a long, slow sip of the strong coffee and thought through the cattle situation once again. "You said you dragged the dead cows up to the barnyard. Where did you find them?"

"Two of them were out by the south gate. I found the other one down by the river."

The river. Up until then, Colt had thought the only thing the ranches who'd lost cows had in common were the cow licks. But now that both Dirk and Paul mentioned it, Colt realized the ranches all bordered Moose Creek! He set his mug on the kitchen counter. "I've got to talk to Doc Moore. I'll call you later." He dashed out into the cold and ran to his Jeep.

On his way back to town, the radio squawked. "Sheriff, this is dispatch. Do you copy?"

He pressed the transmitter. "Yes, Tammy. I copy."

"I just received another complaint about a domestic dispute over at the Munson's'. Neighbors called it in. Again."

"Roger that. I'll stop by when I get back into town." He clicked off the radio and signaled at the next turn.

The Munson's fought like alley cats, but they never really hurt each other. Still, they were loud and frequently upset their neighbors. When Colt was called in, he always ended up feeling like the parent of arguing toddlers. He was sorely tempted to put them in time out until their tempers cooled down.

He parked in front of the single bedroom ranch home, but before he stepped out of the Jeep a cast-iron frying pan flew through the picture window, showering glass into the snow-covered yard.

Ralph Munson ran out of the door wearing an open bathrobe over boxers and a T-shirt. "Did you see that, Sheriff?" He pointed at the house. "That crazy woman is trying to kill me."

"Ralph, if she wanted you dead, she'd have shot you long ago. Now, what's this all about—this time?" Maybe he should arrest them for disturbing the peace and haul them into jail. Pen them up together until they worked through their current argument.

Ralph's wife, Ginger, ran out the door in a flimsy housedress and slippers. "Sheriff, thank God you're here. You need to arrest this idiot and keep him away from me. He tried to choke me! It was all I could do to get away."

"Choke you?" Ralph yelled. "I grabbed your dress when you ran by. How is that choking you?"

"Look. Is there a red mark? My collar almost choked me to death."

Colt saw no marks, red or otherwise. "Okay, you two. Let's go back inside and work this out. No need to give your neighbors a show." Swallowing his own exasperation, he shepherded the angry couple in through the door and closed it behind him.

"Look at this mess, Sheriff. Can you believe what a slob my lazy lump of a husband is? I shouldn't have to clean up this disaster area!"

"No one asked you to," Ralph growled.

Ginger picked up a dirty plate and cocked her arm back as though she was going to throw it at her husband. He flinched and raised his arm to guard his head, and she laughed mockingly. "That's right, you'd *better* duck."

Colt reached for the dish and took it out of her hand. "Sit down, both of you, and stop acting like children. I can't keep getting called out here to settle your arguments. If you truly refuse to get along and no longer want to live together, why don't you separate?"

Both Munson's gawked at him and then glanced at each other. "Well, I don't want to *leave* Ginger, Sheriff. I love her. I just want her to stop screaming at me."

"Well, if you'd clean up after yourself once in a while…" Ginger's fury lost its heat with her husband's admission, and she stared at a spot on the floor.

"Look, I know you both love each other, but you need to learn how to get along. You're driving your neighbors crazy. I think you would benefit from couples counseling, don't you? You need to learn how to communicate."

"We don't need no therapist sticking their nose in our business." Ralph crossed his arms and glared at Colt.

"Yet, it doesn't seem to bother you that your neighbors have a front-row seat to your fights. Listen Ralph, I could arrest you both, haul you into jail, and let a judge order you to get counseling, or you could just call Doc Kennedy and ask him for a recommendation for a therapist and go on your own. What's it going to be?"

"You really think that would help us, Sheriff?" Ginger's eyes searched Colt's face, and his irritation faded.

"It sure couldn't hurt. But for now, let's board up your front window before you both freeze to death." While he and Ralph screwed a sheet of plywood over the broken glass, Colt considered his advice for his own self as well. It seemed he too was constantly struggling to hold it together between Caitlyn and Allison. Maybe they all needed counseling. Why did life have to be so difficult?

18

D irk was on the last flight from New York to Savannah. He thought he'd sleep on the way to Georgia, but a family with a two-year-old sat behind him and the kid cried most of the way. When the bugger wasn't fussing, he was kicking the back of Dirk's seat. Dirk's eyelids weighed heavy over his scratchy eyes by the time he sucked in his first sip of a Venti Americano at the Savannah/Hilton Head International Airport. Instead of renting a car, he ordered an Uber. He might get a few minutes of shut eye before the driver dropped him off at the US Marshals Office located in the downtown historic section of the picturesque southern city.

When the driver stopped at his destination, Dirk pushed his tired frame out of the car and up a set of limestone steps. He entered the building through doors framed by thick Georgian columns. He was pushing on 48 hours without sleep when he entered through security and asked where he could find the Chief Deputy.

With no introduction, Dirk strode into the man's

office. "Dirk Sterling—Montana," he said as he held up the silver-star badge encased in its black-leather holder hanging from a chain around his neck. "I'm going to need a team to help me apprehend Anthony Trova, a fugitive wanted for murder and multiple RICO charges who was last seen in route toward your city. How soon can we go?"

The chief leaned back in his plush, swiveling desk chair and considered him for a moment. "I don't know how ya'll do things up in Montana, Deputy, but we're still civil down here in the south." The man drew out the word south until the vowels were as flat and smooth as the plains of Wyoming.

"Sorry for the lack of niceties, Chief, but I'm tired and more interested in catching a killer."

The man studied Dirk from his seat. "Yes, of course." Dirk smirked at the 'aw' sound that stretched long through the word. "However, all my deputies are off for the evenin' or out of the office on their own cases."

"Can you call someone in? I received notification from the South Carolina State Patrol that the man we've been searching for was seen near here. There has been no further sign of the lux RV he's driving on the highway, so we think he might be camping somewhere on the outskirts of the city."

"Yes... Let me get right on that." Irritation glinted in the man's pale eyes, and he made no move to call anyone. "But, until then, I have a brand-new deputy working in the resource room. He's in the middle of learning the data entry system. I'll have him call around to the *hundred* or so campgrounds in the area and ask if anyone has seen the RV you're looking for."

Dirk clamped his teeth together to keep from offering an unhelpful retort at the chief's sarcasm. Obviously, his rushing into the office and demanding help resulted in this overly polite, passive-aggressive, southern response. But he was in no mood for any bullshit. With that thought, a surge of frustration delivered his angry response, anyway.

"I'm sorry, Chief. I forgot you southerners still think the Civil War is going on, but I'm not a Yankee. I'm from out west, and I need your assistance."

The chief's voice, smooth as molasses—and just as slow—flowed from his thin lips. "I assure you, Deputy Sterling, this has nothing at all to do with the War Between the States. Only that I have coonhounds with more manners than you." He pressed his head back into his chair and crossed his arms.

Dirk bit back his ire and nodded. "Why don't you point me to your rookie deputy."

An imperious and unimpressed brow rose on the chief's forehead, and he pointed to the left. Dirk bobbed his chin and strode from the office. He followed the sound of keyboard clicking to a small room off the main work area containing six empty deputy's desks. Sitting behind an oversized computer screen, was a young man who looked to Dirk like he couldn't be more than thirteen. The new deputies just kept looking younger and younger. The sight of the kid's fresh face made Dirk feel a hundred and one.

He explained his situation to the rookie who nodded as his fingers flew over the keys in a flurry. Within minutes, the newbie had a list of eleven campgrounds who had all registered one or more luxury RV arrivals the past two days. He then made phone calls to the camp hosts with the license plate number Dirk provided. Twenty minutes after Dirk first met the youthful deputy, he was following him out of the building to his car.

On their way past the chief's office, Dirk leaned in. "You'll want to hang on to this kid. He's good."

"We're all good in this office, Deputy Sterling. Don't mistake our slow accent for slow mindedness."

"Oh, I don't, sir. Only for slow action." With that parting shot he pushed through the door and jogged after the young deputy.

They drove to a campground south of town and spoke with the camp host. He led them to the RV in question and Dirk confirmed the license plate number. It was Trova's alright, or at least the RV registered to T&T Holdings.

"They've been parked here for two nights, but I haven't seen either one of them," the host said.

Sterling thanked him, and as soon as the man left, he and the other deputy drew their weapons. Standing to the side of the door, Dirk pounded on the fiberglass. No answer or sound came from inside. He knocked again but only raised the curiosity of the neighboring campers.

Dirk had no warrant, so instead of searching inside the vehicle, he asked everyone he found nearby if the people who owned the huge RV had a second vehicle with them when they arrived, and if so, where they might have gone.

A man returning from a morning of fishing said he'd seen two men leaving the campsite early yesterday morning in a small car. "I figured they were either heading out to shop for food or perhaps some sightseeing, but of course, there's no real way of knowing."

"Did you see the license plate? Or can you describe the car?"

The man pursed his lips. "The car was a beige-colored sedan, but I don't know what kind and I didn't notice the plates at all."

Dirk thanked the fisherman, then dialed Hank who was still at the NYPD offices. "We found the RV with the New York license plates. Does Trova have any holdings or known businesses in Georgia? What about family? I'm wondering if this is just a pit stop, or something more."

"I'll look into it."

"Great. Thanks." Dirk ended the call and spoke to the deputy by his side. "Call in for a warrant. While we wait, our best option is to stake out the RV. They have to come back sometime." His phone buzzed, and he glanced at the screen. He opened a text from Caitlyn. After reading it, he sent her his most recent photo of Anthony Trova.

CAITLYN STARED at the picture Dirk texted her. She was ninety percent certain the man she saw Guillon speaking with at the bar before dinner last night was Anthony Trova. But if so, what was he doing there? How did he and Guillon know each other? Hadn't Dirk said that Trova was on a road trip in an RV with some other *old* guy? Guillon wasn't old. She tossed her phone on the bed and opened the closet in her hotel room. The only item inside was the fancy purple dress she wore last night. She had no outfits to pull off her impromptu undercover identity, but now it was more important than ever that she stay close to Guillon.

Her phone rang and a number she didn't recognize lit the screen. "Hello?"

"Belle. Good morning." It was Guillon.

"Good morning." Caitlyn forced a brightness into her response.

"I'm sending a car for you this afternoon. My driver will escort you from your hotel to my viewing box. I'll see you there. Yes?"

She glanced at her empty closet and bit down on her lower lip. She needed time to go shopping, and she didn't like the idea of being stuck with Guillon's driver. "You're too kind, Guillon, but I'd prefer to drive myself. I want to look in on my horses and check with my jockey. I'm sure you understand. I'll join you before the races start, I promise."

He said nothing for a long minute. Caitlyn knew he wasn't used to anyone saying no to him, and she held her breath. "Am I pushing too hard, ma chérie? Would you rather I leave you alone?"

"No. No, not at all. It's just that it's the first day of the races. I want to be sure Danny has everything he needs, especially my personal encouragement."

"A fortunate jockey, indeed." His voice was low, and he paused. "Fine, then I'll expect you at one o'clock."

"I'll be there."

"Until then." He ended the call.

"Crap, crap, crap!" she yelled. Renegade responded to

her agitation by jumping in circles around her and barking. "Ren, settle down. I need to think." She reached for the room phone and dialed the number for the concierge.

"How may I help you?" A lofty sounding voice answered the line.

Caitlyn made up a story that the airline had lost her luggage and she had no clothes. "I must have some nice things to wear to the races over the next several days, and I need something fast. What do you recommend?"

"I can give you the number to the local Neiman's. You can tell them your sizes and style, and they'll be happy to send a stylist over with some items right away."

"Seriously?" Caitlyn couldn't believe such a service existed, but she covered her astonishment quickly. "I hadn't thought of that. Of course. That's exactly what I'll do. Thank you."

By eleven, Caitlyn's credit card was melting under the strain, but she stood before a full-length mirror in an ivory dress with a navy floral print and matching spectator pumps and hat. She'd pulled her long hair back into a chignon at her nape and pinned the hat to her hair. Renegade watched her from his pile of toys and blankets on the floor.

"What do you think, Ren?" She twirled around before him. He thumped his tail once against the carpet and buried his muzzle between his paws. "Oh, come on. It's not as bad as all that. I think I look kind of nice." She turned to view the back of the dress over her shoulder. "Come on. We've got to get going."

A text buzzed through when they waited for the elevator. It was from Chief Cook: **We've apprehended**

Rutledge. He's willing to testify against Favre in the illegal drug and guns deal.

Caitlyn texted back with a thumbs-up emoji and: **Great news. I need to string Favre along for a little longer until we can nab Anthony Trova. Then we'll have them all. I'll report back soon.**

She and Renegade took an Uber to the racetrack since Danny had driven the truck in earlier, and she and Renegade rushed to the stalls. Danny wore his helmet, its straps hanging unbuckled, and he was sliding into his race silks when they approached.

"Wow, Caitlyn. You're constantly surprising me with your new look. I thought you lost money at the track last time you bet," Danny snickered.

"Yeah, well, you better win today because I have to pay for this getup somehow. I'm expected up in the royal viewing box shortly. Is there someone who can assist you with Triton before his race? Does Neptune need anything?"

"No, and it's not a problem. I'll hire a local groom to help me." He tilted his head and looked her up and down. "You're paying, though. Right?"

"Right. Fine. Just keep your eyes and ears open. Have you heard any gossip about the stolen horses?"

"Nothing so far."

"Well, good luck. I'll see you in the winner's circle!" She grinned at him before she and Renegade left the stables and made their way to the stands.

A uniformed man stood at the base of the stairs leading to the boxes and stopped her when she attempted to move past him. "I'm sorry, Miss. These are private boxes and there are no dogs allowed in the stands."

"I'm a guest of Guillon Favre."

"Sure, and so am I," he snarked. "I'm sorry ma'am. But you'll have to leave the stadium with your dog."

"Is there a problem, Tompkins?" Guillon suddenly appeared behind the man. His complexion deepened, and his eyes bore an implied warning.

"No, sir. I'm just moving a would-be admirer along."

"This woman—and her dog—are my guests for the week. I'm sure you'll see to their ease and comfort."

"Of course. I'm sorry, sir." The guard turned, pink cheeked, to face Caitlyn. "I beg your pardon, ma'am. I didn't know."

She squeezed his forearm. "It's fine. Please, don't feel bad. I'm the one breaking the rules."

The guard stood aside, and Guillon rested his palm on the small of Caitlyn's back, presumably to steady her as she climbed the steps. "There are surely no rules that could contain you, my dear."

Was this guy for real? He sounded like he came out of an old black and white movie. "You're sweet." Renegade tugged on his leash and curled his lip. Clearly, her dog shared her opinion. "*Knoze*, Ren," she murmured, and he stepped to her left side obediently.

When they got to Favre's box, it was empty. "I thought you were expecting a bunch of friends." Apprehension ratcheted up her spine.

"I changed my plans since I desired to be alone with you today. You don't mind, do you?"

"Of course not. I'm honored." She forced a smile and

took her seat at a small table set for two. Immediately, a server appeared with two flutes of champagne. She raised one, and after clinking her glass to Guillon's, she took a tiny sip of the crisp, dry bubbles.

He panned the crowd below. At one point, he paused and inclined his head slightly. Caitlyn followed his line of sight to the man she'd seen him with at the bar the previous night. She pulled her phone from her clutch and pretended to check her appearance in the photo app while secretly snapping a picture. She applied lip gloss and patted her hair while texting the image to Dirk.

Dirk replied instantly: **That's him. I'm on my way.**

Caitlyn's pulse raced, but she kept her expression calm as she slid her phone back into her purse.

Together, she and Guillon ate a light lunch and watched an afternoon of racing. Guillon peered at the track through a small set of binoculars and asked, "Will your uncle be joining you this week?"

For a fraction of a second, Caitlyn wondered why her uncle would be there, but then quickly remembered her impromptu cover as Charles Rutledge's niece. "No. At least not that I'm aware of. I think he's out of the country."

"Oh? Where?

"I'm not sure, actually. Somewhere tropical, I think."

Guillon's gaze bore into her, and he studied her long enough to make her gut squirm. He moved on without more comment, pointing out the many horses belonging to him, and several that belonged to his friends and acquaintances. When Triton pranced out toward his gate behind his lead horse, Caitlyn's chest tightened with excitement. Guillon reached for her hand, but she escaped his hold by jumping to her feet when the starter gun was fired.

She remained standing as she watched Danny maneuver for position. As in the previous race, he held Triton back in fourth place until they were in the backstretch. Caitlyn held her breath. She could tell when Danny released his hold on the colt. Triton's stride opened up, and he surged past the horse in third place, then past second. Caitlyn bounced in her two-toned shoes and squealed when Triton muscled his way into first place as the racers rounded the last bend. He was a nose... then a head... then a full length beyond the horse in second place when he crossed the finish line.

Caitlyn covered her mouth with her hands and whooped into them. Guillon rose beside her and pulled her into is arms. "Congratulations," he said before pressing his lips against hers.

Stunned, she stepped back. She didn't expect that to happen. This guy was too much. Colt would understand though, wouldn't he? She was undercover after all, and Guillon's kiss meant nothing to her.

Guillon responded to the dismay that must have splashed across her face. "I've surprised you. Forgive me. I'll give you more warning the next time I kiss you." He brushed his fingers over her cheek. "Your horse won; you're expected in the winner's circle. Shall I remain here with your dog?"

"Oh. Um. Yes. I guess they won't let him down there, will they?"

He smiled indulgently. "No. I'm afraid not."

Caitlyn bent down and murmured Renegade's Czech

command to stay, not wanting Guillon to wonder why she used foreign words with her dog. She stroked Ren's head and said, "Stay, boy," for the man's benefit before exiting the spectator box and making her way down to the track below.

Looking up at Danny perched on Triton's back, she grinned. "You cost me, you know. I only bet that Triton would show, and I could have won a bundle if I bet on him for the win!"

An arm circled her waist, and she turned. Guillon smiled down at her and kissed her cheek. "Where's Renegade? Did you leave him up in your box?"

"No. I decided I wanted to enjoy this moment with you, so I had my driver walk him over to the stables. He'll be there waiting for you when we're finished here."

An unfamiliar voice called out, "Mr. Favre! Guillon! Over here!" Others joined in calling to Danny as he jumped from Triton's back and stood next to Caitlyn.

With a practiced smoothness used to attention, Guillon turned with her toward the voices and smiled. His perfect features belonged on the cover of GQ. Cameras flashed, and he took the opportunity to ply her with another kiss. This one longer, as if he was publicly staking his claim. Caitlyn did her best to act natural, as though the kiss meant nothing more than congratulations, but the look on Danny's face told her she had failed.

The three posed for photos in front of Triton in the winner's circle before a groom boosted Danny back into the saddle and he walked Triton toward the cool down paddock. From the corner of her eye, Caitlyn noticed a tall, lanky man approach Guillon and whisper something in his ear.

"I must apologize, ma belle," Guillon lifted her chin. "I have an unavoidable business meeting tonight that was scheduled before we met. I cannot escape this obligation, but I shall see you tomorrow. Yes? Same time, same place. Shall I send my driver for you?"

"No. Thank you, though. I'll meet you here. And thank you for a lovely lunch and afternoon." She stepped away and wiggled her fingers in farewell before he had another chance to kiss her. She needed to avoid him if she could and was relieved she wouldn't have to come up with any excuses for dinner or his expectations of dessert. Guillon Favre was not a man who accepted the word no.

19

Caitlyn made her way to the barn in search of Renegade. It surprised her that her dog had gone willingly with the unknown man without making a fuss. When she approached their stables, Neptune was happily munching hay in his stalls and Renegade was in Triton's box, napping.

"Ren?" It was unusual for her high energy dog to sleep when so much activity was going on around him. He didn't stir when she called, so she slid the stall door open and crouched next to him. Running her hand along his side she jiggled him. "Renegade?"

He groaned and opened his eyes a mere slit. His tail flopped lazily in the straw before his lids closed again. "Come on, Ren. It's not time for a nap." She tugged on his collar until he rolled to his stomach. He propped himself up on his forelegs but didn't stand.

Danny's voice echoed through the stable row, and Caitlyn leaned out the door to see where he was. What she saw had her ducking back inside the enclosure. Slowly, she peered around the edge of the opening again. Danny was four stalls down on the opposite side of the aisle, talking to someone she couldn't see inside the stall. They spoke in angry whispers. Danny's face was pinched and red, and he held Triton's reins in one hand while gesturing expressively with the other. He reached into his silk jacket and pulled out a bundle of cash. He thrust it toward the person he was talking to. The man grumbled something, and Danny responded by flinging his arms out in an indignant manner. The action caused Triton to toss his head and sidestep. Danny popped the reins and jammed his free hand onto his lean hip. He closed his eyes and lowered his chin to his chest before nodding. A breath later, he turned and headed toward the stall she was in. Caitlyn continued to watch and seconds later, the man she had seen yelling at Danny from the truck back at Pegasus Farms stepped out from hiding and strode away in the other direction.

Caitlyn wanted to follow him, but when she called to Renegade, he was asleep again. "What is the matter with you, Ren? You're acting like you're hungover." A cold shiver coursed through her as she said the words. "Ren?" Now in full panic, she leaned out the sliding door and yelled down the row. "Is there a vet on site? I need a vet! Now!"

Danny seemed surprised to see her poking her head out of Triton's stall. "What's the matter? Is something wrong with Neptune?" He peered into the second horse's compartment.

"No. It's Renegade." Caitlyn clamped down on the sick

feeling that swam in her belly and the fear she heard in her own voice. She wanted to confront Danny about the altercation she witnessed, but she needed to take care of Renegade first. Something was terribly wrong.

A young woman wearing a hunter green button down with a barn logo stitched on her breast pocket and a stethoscope swinging from her neck hurried toward her. "I'm the vet on staff here. What's the problem?"

"My dog. He's acting lethargic, like he's been drugged or something. Can you tell?"

The vet knelt down and pressed her stethoscope to Renegade's chest, under his arm. "His pulse is within the normal range, maybe a little slow." The vet listened to his breathing before lifting his eyelids and checking his pupil dilation with her penlight. "Has he shown any other symptoms?"

"No. He was fine when I left him about 45 minutes ago. But it's not like him to sleep in the middle of the day, and I can't make him get up." She swallowed against the tremor in her voice. "Is he going to be okay?"

"I specialize in large animals, particularly equine, but from what I can tell he doesn't seem in any distress. I could take some blood and run some basic lab tests?"

"Yes. Please. In the meantime, do you know a local K9 vet you recommend?"

"He's a police dog?"

Caitlyn nodded and opened her clutch purse to reveal her USMS badge. "Please don't mention that I'm a deputy marshal. For now, we need to keep this between the two of us. Okay?"

The woman bobbed her head. "I'll look into this

personally." She took two vials of blood from Renegade's leg without him so much as flinching. When the vet finished, she and Caitlyn exchanged business cards. The doctor gave her a second card with the number of a local vet she said she would consult with. "I'll call you as soon as I know anything. Until then keep a close eye on him. He'll probably sleep it off, but I want you to call me if he has any problems breathing or if he develops any other symptoms. I'll put a rush on the labs. Try not to worry. We'll figure out what's going on."

"Thank you."

Danny helped Caitlyn carry Renegade out of the stall. The groom he hired led Triton into the compartment and began rubbing him down. Danny stroked Renegade's side and without meeting Caitlyn's eye, said, "I figured you'd be going out to dinner with your new high-rolling friends, tonight."

"No." She didn't feel the need to confide in Danny when he was obviously keeping secrets from her. "Did you happen to see who brought Renegade to the stables?"

"No. I was with you—and your boyfriend—in the winner's circle, remember?"

"Yeah, but you got back here before I did. And Guillon is not my boyfriend."

"No, I didn't. I just now brought Triton in from his cool down. You were already here with the vet when I came in. I didn't see anyone else."

Danny was lying to her, but why? He clearly had no idea she'd seen his covert transaction. And it was obvious the unknown man was demanding more money than

Danny had. How much did the jockey owe that guy? Were the stolen horses part of his payment plan? She'd get to the bottom of this, one way or another, but first she needed to take care of Renegade and deal with Favre and his friend. It was hard to comprehend that Anthony Trova was *here* at the Panama City racetrack.

"Listen Danny, Guillon Favre is at Panama Downs in the company of a fugitive we've been chasing for a long time. I need to keep stringing Guillon along until my partner gets here, so I told him I'd go out with him tomorrow night. Lucky for me, he had some important meeting tonight, so I didn't have to spend this evening with him too." She nudged Danny's shoulder playfully. "Besides, I figured you could buy me a celebration dinner with all *your* winnings."

Startled, Danny fumbled for an excuse. "I'm always too tired after a race to go out. I, uh… I was just going to go back to my room and have an early night. And besides, you're married—if you remember—not to mention, I thought you were here to search for the stolen horses, not a boyfriend."

"Of course, I remember I'm married. Look, Danny, my mission has changed. I'm now undercover putting up with Favre so we can catch a fugitive we've been hunting for over a year. None of the flirting means anything to me. And you're right, I was originally here to find the missing horses, but the appearance of our fugitive has changed things.

"About tonight, I figured you and I could order pizza or something simple for dinner. I need to stay with Ren at the hotel and keep an eye on him. I think someone drugged him with something."

Looking relieved, Danny grinned. "Pizza sounds good, but *you're* buying. This is your operation, after all. I'm just here to ride." He knelt to stroke his hand over Renegade's side. "I can help you watch Ren. But why on earth would somebody drug him?"

"I don't know, but it explains why he willingly came here with Favre's guard. Normally, he wouldn't go with someone he doesn't know."

At the hotel, Ren lay on his blankets snoring contentedly, as Caitlyn and Danny polished off a large double-pepperoni and onion pie. Danny left for his room at 9:00. While Caitlyn waited for Dirk to arrive, she FaceTimed Colt. "Hey, how're things going at home?"

"Cold." Colt shivered dramatically. "Is it warm in Florida?"

"Sixties." She smiled. "How was your day?"

"I'm jealous. We could use some sunshine up here. Another local ranch reported three more dead cows and your brother lost another yearling. And, as if my day wasn't bad enough, lucky me, I got to visit the Munson's and settle another one of their domestic explosions. Fun times here. You?"

"Sounds eventful. I'm sorry that Dylan has lost so many cows. That will cost him a lot of money." She curled her legs under her on the couch next to where Renegade slept. "I mostly had a fantastic day." She told him about randomly coming across a man who ended up being Anthony Trova.

"Trova's in Florida? You're kidding me. Is Dirk coming down there?"

"He's on his way. He should get here in an hour or so. Trova is somehow connected to the man who invited me to watch the races from his private spectator's box."

"Be careful, Catie. These are dangerous men."

"I know, and I will be. But I have to admit it's fun going to the races in style. I won $175.00 by betting on Triton to show." She reached down and ran her fingers through Renegade's fur. "The bad news is I think someone slipped Renegade a sleeping pill or something. He's snoozing away and has been for the past couple of hours."

"Is he going to be okay?" Concern filled Colt's voice.

"I think so. I had a vet check him over, and he's not in any stress or danger that she could see. She took some blood and is running some tests, so I'll know what's going on by morning. He's been moving around a little more than before. He wakes up for a few minutes here and there, but then dozes again. He doesn't seem sick, just sleepy. All I'm doing now is monitoring him and waiting for Dirk to get here from Georgia so we can make our move on Trova. Meanwhile, there's something funky going on with Danny." She yawned and rubbed her nose.

"Don't tell me he's connected with Trova, too?"

"No, not that, but I saw him handing a stack of cash to the same man I'd seen yelling at him at the farm a few days ago."

"Where's your ring?"

Colt's question came out of nowhere and temporarily confused her. Then, like a slap across her cheek, she realized her mistake. "Oh. It's in the bathroom. Thanks for mentioning it. I might have forgotten to put it back on before bed."

He considered her through the video screen, and she forced herself not to fidget. With an edged tone, he said, "You didn't say who you sat with in the private spectator's box."

"Oh, didn't I? Sorry. Another horse owner invited me. The guy is friends or is at least doing business with the man I believe to be Anthony Trova. I was hoping Trova would show up with him in the spectator's box today so I could get a closer look, but no such luck. I saw him in the stands though, so I snapped a picture and sent it to Dirk. He confirmed the man is Trova, and now Dirk's on his way down here."

"What's the box-seat guy's *name*?"

She saturated her tone with a nonchalant brightness. "The horse owner? Guillon Favre. Ever heard of him?"

"I don't run in that crowd."

Caitlyn forced a laugh. "Me either. I'm definitely the square peg around here. I fit in at the stable a whole lot better. Favre has three horses here, but they've been in different races than Triton has. These thoroughbreds are so beautiful." She needed to stop jabbering. Colt gave her an odd look, and her belly tightened. The thing was, she felt guilty, even though she had done nothing wrong. She hadn't kissed Guillon. *He* kissed her. Anyway, she'd tell Colt all about her experience when she got home, but it wasn't the kind of story that went very well over the phone.

"Well, go get your ring before you forget to put it back

on. Then I'll tell you about my conversation with Allison today."

Instead of going into the bathroom she dashed to the bureau and snapped open her gold clutch. She found her ring and slid it on. Bouncing back onto the bed, she held up her hand to show him. "Okay, so what's Allison's newest complaint?"

"Same one. She needs a place to live. And if I want to be a regular presence in Jace's life, I need to help her find a home in Moose Creek. She keeps talking about how much cheaper it is to live in Missouri." He paused for her to respond, but when she didn't, he continued. "What do you think about letting her move into the house in town?"

Caitlyn brightened. "Does that mean you've decided that we should live in my cabin permanently? I mean *our* cabin?"

"As much as I'd like that, it's too small. We'd have to build a second bedroom for Jace, and if we don't sell the house in town, we can't afford to build it."

Caitlyn flopped back against her pillow. "What's your plan then?"

"Well, if we sell the cabin, we could buy a bigger home in town. What do you think about that idea?"

"I don't want to live in town, Colt. If I did, I would have bought something there in the first place." Heat swirled in her belly. "Won't the rent we charge Allison be enough to make payments on a construction loan?"

"We can't charge her rent, Catie. Jace is my son."

Caitlyn stared at her husband and tried to swallow the angry words that wanted release. She lost the battle. "Let me get this straight. You want to move your son and *his mother* into your house—rent free—and then make me sell my cabin so you can afford to keep two households?"

"Catie… It's not like that."

"Yeah, well, what's it like then, Colt? You know what? I think we should talk about this when I get home. I'll call you later." She tapped the red button and ended the call.

DIRK HAD no choice but to wait for another team of marshals to show up to keep an eye on the RV before he could have the new deputy drive him back to the airport. Why was Trova at an out-of-the-way racetrack in Florida? He must have flown to Panama City from Savannah because driving would have taken him seven or eight hours. It didn't make sense, but there was no denying that the man in Caitlyn's photo was Trova.

While they waited, the search warrant for the RV came through. The deputy rummaged in his trunk and found a tire-iron. He handed it to Dirk.

"Perfect." Dirk pried the RV door open and both men put latex gloves on before they climbed the stairs and entered the mobile living space. Dirk scanned the interior. "Holy hell, this place is nicer than my house." He gaped at the granite countertops in the kitchenette and the gas fireplace that sat across from the leather couch. The men made their way past a bathroom that included a small washer and dryer to the bedroom in back. A king-sized bed sat proudly in the space, neatly made. Dirk found two shirts hanging in the closet and a few personal items in the bathroom. There was beer in the refrigerator and some chips and crackers in the cupboard, but nothing that gave them any information about the occupants of the RV. Nothing that clued them in on where they were going, or why.

The replacement team arrived, and Dirk texted them a copy of the photo he had of Trova. "Maintain a 24-hour stake out on this RV and keep an eye out for this man. If he shows up, arrest him right away and then call me. I don't have a description of his partner but watch for a second man as well. I've got to fly to Florida, but I'll come right back if you get him."

The rookie drove Dirk back to the Savannah airport where he hopped a Delta flight to Panama City. He caught twenty minutes of sleep in-flight, but it wasn't enough. He hadn't pushed this hard since he was a grunt in the Marine Corps.

As soon as Dirk got off the plane, he rented a car and tossed his duffle bag into the back seat. He programmed Caitlyn's hotel into his GPS which informed him he'd be there in half an hour. He tried her phone, but it sent him to voicemail. No matter, he'd rather talk to her in person, anyway.

On his way through the hotel lobby, he tipped his cowboy hat to the desk clerk and strode directly to the elevators.

Caitlyn opened her room door on his second knock. "It took you long enough." She wore a thin, faded Wyoming Cowboys T-shirt and what looked like a pair of men's boxers. He kept his gaze off her long bare legs and firmly on her face. Renegade snored peacefully on the bed behind her.

"I got here as fast as I could. I left a deputy with an NYPD detective in Manhattan to keep watch on Trova's family so I could chase him down to Savannah. And now he shows up here."

"I'm glad I was able to sneak a picture of him. I would have taken more today, but Favre kicked everyone out of his box so we could be alone." She used air quotes and rolled her eyes.

"He likes you, huh? We can work with that."

"That's what I thought, but his interest only has value if it gets us closer to Trova."

"Any idea why Trova is here in Florida?" Dirk dropped his duffle in the corner of the room. "Did you notice anyone else with him? Maybe a guy about his same age? Or a little older?"

"I don't know... I don't think so. I saw him at the bar, and once at the track. Both locations were crowded, so I can't be sure."

"Trova is supposedly on some road trip with a buddy. But that could be false information. We found his RV dumped off at a campground in Savannah. He must have flown down here from there. The guy is slippery."

Caitlyn sat next to her dog and stroked his head. "He won't suspect we're looking for him in Florida. We're so close, I can taste it."

"Aren't you supposed to be working a different case? And what's up with Renegade? He never sleeps through my grand entrances."

Caitlyn told him what she suspected about Favre's guard drugging Ren. "Maybe he was difficult to handle, and the guy didn't want to deal with him or something. I don't know, but the vet thinks he'll be fine and just needs to sleep it off. As far as the Tennessee case goes, I'm working on that while I'm down here, too. The jockey, Danny Franco, who's riding for Pegasus Farms is in some sort of financial trouble. I witnessed him paying off some guy, and I can't help but think Danny might have made it possible for the midnight horse thieves to steal those horses out of the barn. Perhaps they were partial payment for whatever he's gotten himself into."

"I guess we're getting a front-row view of the seedy underbelly of the racing world." Dirk eased into a chair by the desk. "So, what's the plan for tomorrow?"

"I'm invited to watch the races with Favre again, so I'll be on scene if Trova shows up. If he doesn't, I'll ask Guillon about him and see if I can unearth any information. But if he's there, I'll text you and you can swoop in and finally nab him."

"It's been a long time coming." Dirk hoped they were right about the man Caitlyn saw. She'd never actually seen Trova in person, and the pictures he'd sent her were either twenty-years old, or of Trova's face in the shadows. He opened the recent photo she'd texted him and studied it again. It was shadowy, but it looked enough like Trova to get Dirk to fly down there.

"So, who's watching the horse farm in Tennessee? I thought they assigned you to that job so you could ease back into work."

"They did, but I can't help it if things got hot." Her grin filled with mischief. "Besides, once the Nashville Chief Deputy realized racing the horses could be financially beneficial to his office, he was all about it."

Dirk shook his head. "I'm not sure if *you* find trouble, or *it* finds you, but one thing I know is you're always in the thick of it. I'm going to go get a room and snag some much needed sleep, but I'll be in the stands tomorrow. I hope Renegade is back on his feet by then."

At the mention of his name, Renegade's tail flopped up and down on the bed, but his eyes remained shut.

20

Colt bent forward and rested his forehead against his folded arms on his desktop. He hadn't slept well after his argument with Caitlyn. She could be so stubborn. Couldn't she see that he was straddling an electric wire? If he didn't give Allison an offer she couldn't refuse, she'd take Jace out of his life. Then again... he had to admit he could have been more sensitive to his wife's feelings. He should have handled the whole conversation better. It's just that Caitlyn had acted weird about that rich French dude, and the fact that she wasn't wearing her wedding ring threw him off his game. He'd call her after work and apologize. He agreed they should talk about all this in person, but Allison was pressuring him, and he was afraid she'd leave before he could stop her.

The office door swung open, and a cold breeze jolted him out of his tumultuous thoughts. "Sleeping on the job?" Allison's saccharin voice bit into his nerves. Her flowery perfume punched him in the nose, and the oatmeal he'd eaten for breakfast turned into a brick in his belly.

"Just resting a minute. I didn't get much sleep last night. What do you want, Allison?"

"That's not a nice way to greet someone." She pouted.

"Is everything okay with Jace?"

"Yes." She waved a hand at him as though sweeping the mention of their son away. "I just stopped by to congratulate you. I didn't know you and Caitlyn owned a racehorse."

He scrunched his brows down. "What are you talking about?"

She blinked her eyes at him and smiled like a well-fed feline. "This, of course, silly." She snapped open a tabloid newspaper and laid it across his desk. There in a colored half-page spread was his wife, kissing some other man. The headline read: **Lucky in Love and in the Races!** The article went on to say, "Caitlyn Rutledge, niece of Charles and Tansey Rutledge wins big at Panama Downs, and not just on the track. It seems she's caught the eye and won the heart of billionaire Guillon Favre as well." Allison smirked at Colt. "I don't know why she's using the last name Rutledge, but it sure looks like you're in the money. So... about finding me a place to live?"

Colt couldn't breathe, and he didn't dare move. If he did, he might strangle the woman staring at him with sick satisfaction. He reached for the paper and bunched it in his fist. Swallowing hard and drawing a deep breath in through his nose, he said, "Yeah. I was going to call you later this afternoon. I'll be moving the remaining things out of my house in town this weekend, and I thought you and Jace could move in there."

"Oh. Well, how much will the rent be? You shouldn't have to charge me very much. I'm sure you own that old shack outright, and with all the race winnings coming in..."

"The first month will be rent free. Then after Catie gets home, we'll discuss it and make sure we price your rent at a fair amount."

"Are you sure she's coming home?" Allison's smug expression spurred his anger.

He wanted to tell her to put her fangs away, but he didn't dare risk making her angry. He had to play nice until he had his 50/50 parenting order from the court. And the truth was, he didn't know what the hell was going on with Caitlyn. But that was between them, and none of Allison's business. "I'll move my stuff out this week, and then I can help you two move in on Saturday, if that works for you."

She slid around his desk and rested her manicured hand on his biceps. "I look forward to spending the day with you and Jace, the three of us together. I'll pack a lunch."

He moved away. "Sounds like a plan, but for now, I've got work to do."

She perched her hip on the corner of his desk. "Need any help?"

The office phone rang, and he snatched up the receiver. "Sheriff's office. Branson here." Colt turned his back to Allison to create a little privacy for his call.

"Sheriff, it's Doctor Moore. I believe I've discovered the reason those cows are dying."

"What did you find?"

Dr. Moore cleared his throat. "I got the results of the blood tests, and the toxicology reports show two foreign chemicals found in all the dead cows."

"Which chemicals?"

"Acetone and lithium. But I can't imagine how cows from all around the county ended up with those chemicals in their blood."

"I have an idea. I meant to call you yesterday, but I had to deal with a few other things. Could those chemicals be distributed through water?"

"Yes. In fact, that's the most probable vehicle."

"It occurred to me that Moose Creek borders or runs through the properties of all the different ranches that have lost cows. Every one of them has river access."

"Then we need to test that water immediately."

"Let's meet out at Reed Ranch and test the water there. I'll have my deputy call all the ranches along the river and tell them to keep their livestock away from the water for the time being. At least until we determine if the chemicals are coming from Moose Creek."

"Good. I'll be on my way as soon as I gather my testing tools."

Colt's mind tugged at his memory. Those two chemicals together pointed to something, but he couldn't remember what. He stuffed his phone into his pocket and grabbed his keys from the desk. When he turned to leave, he almost bumped into Allison. He'd forgotten she was still there. "I have to go."

"What's going on? Did you say there are poisonous chemicals in the river?" Allison held her ground.

Colt moved around her and put his coat on. "We don't know for sure, but we're looking into it." He settled his dove-colored cowboy hat on his head and reached for the door. "Please keep this to yourself until we know what we're dealing with, okay?"

Allison gripped his arm. "I can help Wes call the ranches, if you want."

"No, thanks. It's an official message that needs to come from this office. I'll see you later." With that he left Allison standing by his desk, and he called Wes on his way to his Jeep.

———————

21

Caitlyn, wearing her running shoes which were completely out of sync with her red-jersey afternoon dress and red-and-black fascinator hat, hopped out of the truck and led Renegade to Triton and Neptune's stables. She'd had to carry her dog to the truck from the hotel, but fortunately, he seemed a little more with it once they arrived at the track. He followed her to the stalls on his own four feet.

Danny sat outside the pens on a bale of hay, chewing gum and reading the *Thoroughbred Daily*. He glanced up as she approached. "Renegade's okay, then?" He folded the paper and tucked it under his leg. "Ever figure out what was wrong?"

Her dog sat when she stopped in front of the jockey. "He's doing better, but he's still a bit groggy. I haven't heard from the vet yet." She handed Ren's leash to Danny. "Will you hang on to him for a minute? I've got to change my shoes before I go up to Guillon's box." She kicked off her sneakers and pulled a pair of black, patent leather pumps and a matching purse out of her backpack.

"You're covered in dog hair, you know." Danny plucked a clump of tawny hair from her skirt.

"I had to carry him, and now I'm a mess." Caitlyn brushed at the hair on her dress, but it didn't help. "I can't go to the spectator's box looking like this."

"I have some duct tape in the tack chest." He rummaged in the box and found the roll.

Caitlyn pulled off a length of tape and tore it with her teeth. She wrapped a loop around her hand and wiped her dress again. "You're a lifesaver, Danny. Thanks." She glanced at her watch knowing she'd have to run to make it in time to see Guillon's horse in the first race of the day. "Come on Ren, we've got to hurry."

Renegade dragged against her pace, and she paused at the bottom of the steps to the grandstand. She needed a few seconds to slow her breathing before she and Renegade made their way up the final stairs to their seats. The usher opened the door for them. Guillon stood in a summer-weight linen suit, and he greeted her as she and Renegade entered the box. He tipped his straw fedora and took her hand but hesitated before leading her to her seat. "You have a clump of... dog hair on your shoulder, my dear."

"Oh, thanks" She brushed it away and glanced around. "Will your friends be joining us today?"

"Yes, along with several business associates. It's a big day at the races for all of us. In fact, I saw that your horse, Triton, is in the lineup with my horse, Normandy Star, in the second race of the day, after lunch. Perhaps we should make a friendly wager?"

"What did you have in mind?" Caitlyn gave him a suggestive smile that he returned in kind. He slid his hands around her waist, but before he had a chance to show her what he had in mind, the door opened again, and a group of handsomely dressed people entered the box.

The women were swathed in dresses that likely cost more than Caitlyn made in a month. And their hats were clearly designed specifically to coordinate with their purses and shoes. The men were turned out equally well, though more understated in their light colored suits and ties. Caitlyn felt as though she'd stepped back into a much more elegant era, one that if she had lived in, she'd have certainly been a servant, not a lady dressed in silk. She didn't belong in this group of people, and she only hoped she could fake it convincingly enough to avoid suspicion until she found Trova.

One of the men made his way to Guillon's side and shook his hand. Guillon introduced him to Caitlyn as Max Wentworth. The newcomer lifted her hand with soft fingers and smiled lasciviously, winking at Guillon. "And how did *you* come to meet The Banker, Ms. Rutledge?"

"Pardon?" Caitlyn asked. Hadn't Danny mentioned a man called The Banker? Her pulse leapt but she kept her expression passive as she looked up at Guillon.

Favre's complexion darkened at the use of the moniker. "A silly nickname from our school days." He turned her away from the man, dismissing him. "Do not go near Wentworth," he murmured in Caitlyn's ear. "He's a lech."

As more spectators filed in, Guillon introduced her to them, and she quickly realized Trova was not among them. "Will your friend, the man you were with the night we met at the bar, be here today?" Caitlyn did her best to sound casual, but Guillon's eyes narrowed.

His brows dipped in question. "Why do you ask?"

The bugler saved Caitlyn by playing "First Call," announcing the beginning of the race. Pretending to be distracted, she held a small pair of binoculars to her eyes. "The first race is starting. Do you have any horses in this one?" But instead of viewing the horses at the gate, she panned the crowd below searching for Dirk. When she spotted him, she slowly shook her head no to signal that Trova wasn't there, yet. Dirk touched the brim of his hat to let her know he got her message.

Guillon scanned his race program. "Yes, my filly, Deauville." He pointed to the name in the lineup. As they watched the horses and riders get ready, Guillon rested his hand on the small of Caitlyn's back and pointed. "Deau is in gate number four. I have a good feeling about this race." A broad smile smoothed across his handsome face.

The starting shot fired, and the horses leapt from the starting gates. Hooves pounded frantically, kicking up sand from the track, and Caitlyn found herself holding her breath. A dark brown filly called Breezy Bay bolted into the lead immediately. The following horses remained clumped together, their jockeys clamoring for position. By the time the racers were in the backstretch, four horses led the pack. Breezy Bay held the lead by two lengths.

Caitlyn watched the race through her field glasses. "Look at Breezy go! No one will catch her now."

"We'll see." Guillon's hand slid around Caitlyn's waist, and his grip tightened.

The young horses flew around the final turn. Suddenly, Breezy Bay faltered, and she lost her edge. Her stride shortened, and the two horses in closest pursuit caught up to her. Still, she slowed, falling back into fourth. In the final outcome, Guillon's filly, Deauville, came in first, followed closely by a black colt named Jumeirah. Breezy Bay had dropped all the way back to 7th place.

"I won!" Guillon drew Caitlyn into an embrace and kissed her, but in his excitement he didn't linger. Maintaining his hold on her, he threw his other fist into the air. "I won!"

"Congratulations, Guillon! Hurry, now. They'll want you in the winner's circle." Caitlyn pushed him toward the door.

"Come with me." He took hold of her hand.

"Me? No. I don't belong down there with you. I should stay up here with Renegade."

"Of course, you belong. Leave Renegade here. He's taking a nap." Guillon pulled on her hand.

Renegade's head rested on his front paws as he watched her from the top of his eyes. Favre led Caitlyn down the steps to the ground level and out to the winner circle where they joined his victorious horse and jockey.

"I'm so pleased for you," Caitlyn said as he held her tight to his chest.

"Me too. I just won a great deal of money. I bet on Deauville to win!"

"I wonder what happened to the horse that was in the lead? She really fell back. I'm glad your horse won, but I hope that filly is okay."

"She'll be fine, I'm sure." Guillon's eyes held a peculiar glint that gave Caitlyn reason to wonder. "But right now, I'm not worrying about it. Now is the time for us to celebrate!"

DIRK WOKE EARLY THAT MORNING. He'd entered his hotel room the night before and dropped onto the bed, falling asleep with his boots on. His hot morning shower felt better than anything and he'd stood under it for twenty minutes before he started his day.

When he got to the track, he'd blended in with the crowd and wandered the grounds until he was comfortable with his surroundings. He located all the bathrooms and exits and surveyed the people in the casino while managing to lose less than thirty bucks in the slot machines.

When the stands started to fill, Dirk made his way there. Casually, he glanced up at the private boxes filled with the wealthy. Women were dressed to the nines with matching flamboyant hats and the men wore suits and straw fedoras. He located Caitlyn, but let his gaze travel past her without landing, as though he were merely scanning the crowd. He strolled from one end of the grandstand to the other until he found a strategic location.

Dirk stood with his back against a cement support beam. He angled his head so that it appeared he was looking down at the track when in truth, he was watching Caitlyn and Favre in their spectator's box from behind his mirrored glasses. Favre was behaving awfully familiar with Caitlyn. He was constantly touching her, which was like sticking your hand unknowingly into a rattlesnake hole. Dirk smirked to himself. If Favre didn't watch out, he would find that out the hard way.

The starting gun sounded, and the horses bolted from the gate, but Dirk kept his eyes on Caitlyn. The race was over within a minute or so and Favre's horse must have won. Either that, or he'd made big on a bet. Dirk's jaw muscles tightened as he watched the man pull Caitlyn into his arms and kiss her on her mouth. He thought, *I hope you know what you're doing, Reed.* The kind of men that Trova associated with were not the type to be trifled with.

Dirk realized Favre's horse won the race when he and Caitlyn worked their way down to the winner's circle. Renegade wasn't with her, and he hoped Caitlyn's dog was okay. Maybe she left him in the barn with the jockey. All Dirk knew, was he'd feel much better if Ren was by her side.

22

Colt stopped by Dylan on the road when he drove into the barnyard at Reed Ranch and rolled down his window. "Get in. We need to drive down to the river." Dylan hurried around the hood and jumped in the passenger side. "Doctor Moore should be here any minute."

"He's already here. He said to meet him down by the creek. What's going on?" Dylan's dark eyes bore into Colt. "Is this about what's killing the cattle?"

Colt explained how Doctor Moore found two specific chemicals in the blood tests he performed on each of the dead cows. "I didn't remember right away, but on my way over here it occurred to me that both acetone and lithium are used in the production of methamphetamine."

"There's meth in the river?" Dylan's brows knit together in confusion, and he cocked his head.

Colt turned onto the rough two-track path made by farm vehicles and drove through the pastures toward Moose Creek. "No, not meth exactly, but the toxic chemicals cookers use, along with several others, to make meth. Even if that isn't the case here, I'm pretty sure those chemicals are what's killing the cattle."

"Thank God I moved my herd up closer to the barn. They're drinking from a trough connected to the well." Dylan's eyes widened and his mouth dropped open. "You don't think the well water is contaminated too, do you?"

"I doubt it, but everyone along the river should have their well water tested just in case." The thought caused Colt's stomach to knot.

Dylan pulled out his phone. "Kenze, listen. Do not drink or use any water from the house. If you need to, go into town and buy some water for drinking and cooking." He paused and listened to his wife's response. "There might be toxins in the water. It's likely not a problem, but for now let's take precautions. And yes, even for the dogs. And will you turn off the water to the house and barn until I call you back?"

"Hopefully that's overkill, but it's not a bad idea." Colt called Wes again and relayed the same safeguards. "Call all the ranchers along the river and make them aware of the situation."

Colt parked next to Doctor Moore's mobile-vet truck, and they met him at the river's edge. Moose Creek was frozen over in spots, but water rippled swiftly underneath the ice. The scene was peaceful, and Colt had a hard time getting his mind around the idea that such clear water could be lethal.

Doctor Moore looked up when the men approached. "I'm taking several samples here, and I will do the same tests at each of the ranches that have lost cattle."

"Isn't it all the same water?" Dylan crouched next to the vet.

"Yes, and no. There might be greater concentrations in some areas than in others."

Colt stood with his hands on his hips. "This is probably a job for the EPA."

"Yes. That's likely." The vet screwed a lid onto a glass jar filled with icy creek water.

"How could those chemicals get into the river?" Dylan asked. "Colt said they're used to make meth, but I still don't get it. Why would they be in the creek?"

Doctor Moore shrugged and glanced over at Colt. He nodded. "I had the same thought. I'll call the EPA and get someone up to the reservoir to test the town's water supply immediately."

"Dylan, you and I should take a couple of horses and ride up the river toward Moose Lake. We'll see if we can find anything that might be leaking the toxins into the creek along the way. Doc, keep me posted as to what you and the EPA find out at the reservoir. We could have a town-wide crisis on our hands."

Dylan jogged toward Colt's Jeep. "Let's go."

Colt drove them to the barn where they both donned warm winter coveralls. They saddled Sampson and Whiskey and set out to look for any clues of how the chemicals had seeped into the river their entire town relied upon.

Sun glittered off the snow in a blinding light through Colt's mirrored sunglasses. If it wasn't for his worry and concern for the town, he would have reveled in the pristine mountain scenery. The fresh air was so crisp and cold that ice crystals formed on the tips of Dylan's mustache and the horses' whiskers from their frozen puffs of breath. Snow covered the landscape and deadened all sound. Except for the occasional hawk crying out in flight, a peaceful silence surrounded them.

They had left the Reeds' land miles ago and were now traveling along the Bureau of Land Management property owned by the federal government. This high up, the mountains were mostly untouched by man and his idea of progress. Colt had always loved being up on the range and the thought that someone had sullied the purity of the water burned in his throat.

Dylan halted Sampson and twisted in his saddle to face Colt. "We're only about fifteen miles from the lake, and so far, we've seen nothing that indicates the source of the chemicals. Have you heard from Doc Moore?"

Colt checked his satellite phone. The battery was low due to the cold temperature. "Nothing yet. But the EPA will test everything when they get to Moose Creek, including the reservoir water and water from the treatment facility." He turned the phone off to conserve the little charge he had left.

Dylan pushed Sampson forward. "If we get all the way to the lake before we find anything, I'll have McKenzie bring the trailer and pick us up."

Colt nodded, not sure whether he'd rather find something sooner than not at all. They reached a meadow, and Colt nudged Whiskey into a slow trot until the terrain changed and made for slow going once again. They rode in silence, each leaving the other to their own thoughts. Colt sorted through the steps he'd have to take in response to a chemical disaster in his little town, while at the same time praying he wouldn't have to go that far.

Another five miles up the river, and Colt could no longer feel his toes. He tugged his scarf tighter around his neck and pressed on. A sharp glare of light flashed at him from beyond the next stand of pines. "Do you see something through those trees?"

Dylan halted his horse and stared in the direction Colt pointed. "No. Did you?"

"Something flashed in the sun. Let's check it out." He squeezed Whiskey's sides, and they trotted to the edge of the thick group of pines. He dismounted and looped his reins over a low branch. "I can't ride through this thicket, but I'll go in on foot and look around."

Dylan jumped down from his horse and followed Colt through the trees. When they came out the other side of the stand, they saw a shack with an unpainted tin roof. Colt pointed. "That's what must have reflected the sunlight. Whose shed is this? Aren't we still on BLM?"

"Yep. We haven't come to the boundary fence yet, so we're still on government land. I don't know who built this, but it's illegal to build personal structures on BLM property without a government permit."

"Well, somebody did. This rickety structure isn't built with an eye toward any building codes." Together, they approached the door. It was locked shut with a padlock. They walked around the shack and found a PVC pipe leading from the hut out toward the river. "This doesn't look good." Colt reached inside his coat for his sat phone. "I'm calling for a warrant. I want to see what's inside." He turned on the phone, glad to see he still had some charge left on the battery. He tapped on the device. "I must be in a dead zone."

"What do you mean a dead zone? I thought you could use a sat phone anywhere." Dylan peered over his shoulder.

"It happens."

Colt and Dylan followed the PVC pipe down the hill to the edge of a cliff thirty feet above Moose Creek. From there, whatever was draining from the shack would pour into the water below. "The ground all down this cliffside could be contaminated." Dylan rubbed his mouth with his gloved hand. "I wonder what the clean-up procedure for something like this entails?"

"If this is where the toxic chemicals are coming from—and I'm sure it is—we'll have to call in a HAZMAT team." Colt rubbed the back of his neck. He tried his phone again, but it was still searching for a signal. He tromped fifty yards through the snow to a clearing and tried again. "Damn! Still no signal." It was too cold for this. He turned to the south, trudged another thirty feet and this time pulled his hand from his glove exposing his fingers to the freeze. He pressed the buttons and stared at the olive-green screen. Finally, his call to the county judge's office went through.

Colt stood shivering where he was, enduring the bitter wind blowing through the trees, while they waited for the necessary documentation to come through. Twenty minutes later, he received the text message which allowed him to enter the premises. The men hiked back to the flimsy building.

Colt clapped Dylan on the shoulder. "You need to go wait for me by the horses."

"I'm not letting you go in there alone."

"Dylan, I'm not asking." Colt fished in his coat pocket and pulled out a bandana. "I'll cover my mouth and nose before I open the door, as a precaution. But I'm not breaking the lock until you're out of here."

Dylan grumbled something unintelligible, but he backed up to the edge of the trees. He refused to go any farther. Colt approached the opening. He found a rock big enough to break the lock and smashed it against the metal latch. It swung up and down but it didn't break. It took Colt three swings before the lock broke apart. Slowly, he pushed the plywood door. It creaked on rusty hinges as it swung inward.

Inside the hut, on a temporary table made from sawhorses and a slab of wood, stood a stock of supplies that looked like they came from the high-school chemistry department. There were a couple of Bunsen burners attached to a propane tank, several beakers and glass pitchers, plastic tubing, and buckets. On a shelf above the table were all the telltale ingredients. Jugs of Drano and muriatic acid, tin cartons of acetone, and bottles of ammonia sat next to ten or more boxes of nasal decongestant, a bottle of Heet, a respirator, and a space heater.

Against the back wall, on the floor, was a sleeping bag and a backpack stuffed with clothes. A box holding a box of crackers, a jar peanut butter, some bags of snack items sat next to a thermos and a hotplate with a small saucepan. Whoever was mixing the chemicals, also lived there, at least part of the time. He didn't need to see anymore.

Colt backed out of the shack and closed the door. He walked to where Dylan stood waiting. "It's definitely a meth lab." He grimaced. "We've got to seal this place off until a HAZMAT team can get up here to clean it up."

"Is there anything we can do to stop the contamination right now?"

"Fortunately, nothing is draining into the creek at the moment, but touching, or even breathing, any of this could be deadly. We'll let the professionals handle it. At least we know what's been poisoning the river and that the lake should be clean."

Colt scraped the message "Poison. Stay Out!" on the plywood door. He retrieved a zip-tie from a pouch on his gun belt and slid it through the latch that had held the padlock and tightened it down. "We'll need to get a team up here right away. I'm sure they can land a helicopter in the small meadow we came through. But for now, let's get out of here."

On the return trip to the ranch, Colt told Dylan about all the supplies he'd seen inside the shack.

Dylan guided his horse around a boulder. "Who would build a meth lab so far away from civilization?"

"Who knows. Maybe they only work it in the summer months when they can hike up here."

"We could camp out and watch to see who comes back. Catch them in the act."

"I'd love to catch the cookers red-handed, but we can't waste time staking out the place. It's too dangerous to leave all those chemicals sitting there. They're highly flammable and even in the winter, could cause a forest fire."

"How will you catch them, then?"

"I'm not sure if we ever will."

It was late afternoon when they rode up to the Reeds' barn. McKenzie was struggling to carry a big jug of water into the kennel, and Dylan jumped from his horse to take the load from her arms. He told her what they'd found.

"Too bad Renegade isn't here," McKenzie followed him to the building. "He and Caitlyn could have tried to track the dirtbags."

"It's snowed since they were last there. There weren't any tracks." Dylan set the water inside the door of the kennel building and went to get another jug from his wife's car.

She held the door open for him. "The snow is less of a problem than time. It really depends on how old a trail is."

"The biggest problem right now is getting that toxic mess taken care of and keeping the town safe." Colt handed Whiskey's reins to Dylan. "Mind putting him away for me? I need to call Doctor Moore and HAZMAT. I want to organize the cleanup as soon as possible."

It was dusk when Colt headed home. When he turned onto the mountain highway, the back end of his Jeep fish-tailed on the slick tarmac and doused his system with adrenaline. He sucked in a gulp of air and downshifted to slow his vehicle rather than use his brakes on the ice. Under his breath, he mumbled a curse for not being able to get back to town any faster. Now was not the time for snow and ice.

On his way down the canyon, an idiot in a beat-up,

two-door hatchback raced up behind him, riding his tail. Colt downshifted again, to make the point of slowing down. The driver of the small car flashed his headlights and crept closer. He obviously was unaware he was harassing a Sheriff's vehicle. Colt held his crawling pace.

Eventually, the hatchback passed him, blaring his horn as he sailed by, brazenly crossing the double yellow centerline. Colt made a mental note of the car's license plate number.

The grade steepened as they approached a set of hairpin turns. The car in front of him braked and slipped on the ice before correcting, and Colt noticed the left brake light hadn't come on.

That's it. Strike three. Colt flipped on his flashing lights and tapped his siren. The vehicle sped up. "Don't be an ass. You're gonna end up driving off the road and killing yourself," he said out loud.

The smaller car slid close to the edge on the next turn, and the driver must have realized he would not escape being pulled over. He slowed down and stopped as soon as there was enough room on the shoulder of the highway to pull over. Dusk deepened the shadows in the canyon, and Colt clicked on his high beams along with the flood-light attached to his door. He pulled in behind the compact, leaving one car length between them and pointing the nose of his Jeep slightly outward. He canted his front tires to the left.

Colt called Tammy in Dispatch. "I've stopped Wyoming plate 18 739 on the mountain highway, at mile-marker 71." She repeated the information back to him for confirmation. Colt stepped out of the Jeep, closing his door softly. He approached the driver's side, placing his bare hand on the back hatch when he walked by.

As he got closer, he bent to peer in through the window, watching the driver carefully. His brain took less than a second to assess who the man was, and that he held a gun. *Burroughs!* Colt gripped the handle of his own weapon and yanked it from its holster. A gunshot echoed against the rock walls of the canyon. Colt dove to the ground and fired a round back at Burroughs.

The hatchback's engine whined, and the responding tires spit gravel and ice into Colt's face as it raced away, careening down the treacherous canyon road.

———

23

After Guillon charmed the press and photographers took all the winner circle photos, he guided Caitlyn back toward the stands. They made their way up through the ticketed seats to his private box and found a light and refreshing lunch laid out on the tables, waiting to be served.

"Champagne first!" Guillon gestured to the server who began filling flutes for the guests.

Caitlyn's phone buzzed, vibrating in her small clutch. The name on the caller ID identified the racetrack vet. "Hello, this is Caitlyn R—." She stopped short of saying her last name.

"Yes, Deputy Reed. I'm calling with the toxicology report on your dog. Strangely, his labs show the presence of Xylazine in his blood. That's a drug used to tranquilize horses."

Caitlyn stepped away from Guillon and lowered her voice. "How could that be? Is that something he could have found on the ground and ingested? How much did he have?"

"I don't see how he could have gotten into the drug. It's a prescription medicine, and it's injected, not swallowed."

"Injected? Is Renegade in danger?"

"To be honest, the tranquilizer can cause dogs to swallow an excess amount of air and bloat. Often this causes vomiting. Did he display any of those symptoms?"

"Now that you mention it, his belly has been a little distended."

"How was his breathing through the night?"

Caitlyn rolled the corner of her lip between her teeth. "At times, he sounded like he was gulping air, but then he'd settle down. It was a fitful night."

"Sometimes we give Naloxone for a Xylazine overdose, but it sounds like Renegade's seen the worst of it already. I think it's best if we don't give him any more medicines. He may be sleepy for the rest of the day. Malinois have such high metabolisms which likely caused him to burn through the drug faster than usual. And that may have saved his life."

Caitlyn shivered with an icy fury. Who would do such a thing to her dog? Obviously, Guillon's man had something to do with it. But why? And where did he get the tranquilizer if a prescription was required? She glanced behind her to check on Guillon's location before she asked the vet, "Is it common to have Xylazine sitting around the stables?"

"We keep it on hand in case we need to treat a high-strung horse for an injury. It ensures the safety of both the animal and the doctor. But as I said, it's a prescription medication, so you should only find it in a veterinarian's possession."

"Did you check to see if you were missing any of yours?"

"Yes, and I am not. I have a full, unopened bottle in my bag."

"Thanks, Doc. I'll call if I have any more questions."

"Please keep me posted. How is Renegade doing today, by the way?"

"He's still not himself, but he seems a little less groggy than before."

"Make sure he has plenty of water," the vet advised before she ended the call.

Guillon was watching her with hooded eyes. "Who was that?"

Caitlyn slipped her phone into her handbag. "That was the racetrack veterinarian I asked to examine Renegade. She was checking on him. She told me the lab found evidence of Xylazine, a horse tranquilizer, in his blood. I'm trying to think of who could have given it to him... and why? The only other person Ren was with besides me was your driver. You don't think *he* drugged Renegade, do you?"

The muscle of Guillon's jaw worked before he answered. "Of course not. Why would he do such a thing?"

"I don't know. Maybe he was afraid of my dog? Perhaps he thought if Renegade was calmer, he'd be easier to handle. Could you ask him?"

"Certainly, but I already know the answer. What about

your jockey? He's spent more time with your dog than anyone else besides you, hasn't he?"

"Not alone. Not really." Caitlyn ran her mind over the past days. She supposed it was possible that Danny was involved, but what reason would he have? And when would he have had the opportunity?

A local celebrity called, "Riders Up!" over the microphone, interrupting her thoughts. The jockeys got their leg up and rode their hot-blooded horses past the grandstands, eliciting cheers from the excited crowd. A moment later the bugler played the "Call to the Post," and the riders made their way toward the starting gate.

"Let's talk to him about it, later." Guillon pointed to the gate. "The horses are lining up."

"This is Triton's and Normandy's race." Caitlyn stood on her toes to see the horses over the crowd.

Guillon leaned into her, his breath causing bumps to rise on her neck. "Yes. And we still need to discuss our friendly wager."

Caitlyn moved away to check on Renegade and to create space between her and Guillon. Ren's breathing was still normal, and though he seemed to be snoozing, he flopped his tail against the floorboards when she stroked his head. "Good boy, Ren. You'll be feeling better soon."

"Hurry, my dear. The race will start any second." Guillon held his hand out to her, and she allowed him to help her up.

Caitlyn lifted a small set of binoculars to her eyes. She panned down the row of jockeys as they loaded into the starting gate until she found Danny astride Triton. Next to the riders were members of the gate crew helping load the horses. Sunlight flashed off something in the man's hand who was assisting with Triton, but Caitlyn couldn't make out what it was. Moving her gaze down the row, she saw Normandy prancing in place behind gate number two.

Even though she was technically working, Caitlyn couldn't help but bubble up with excitement. She'd placed a hundred-dollar bet on Triton to win. It seemed that no other horse at Panama Downs this week could catch him. Bells sounded and the starting shot fired. The gates swung open, and fifteen horses bolted forward onto the track. They bunched toward the inside rail and gradually found their positions. Triton was at the front of the pack with two other horses. He battled with a chestnut colt called Time to Fly, and Normandy Star, for the lead.

"Go Triton!" Caitlyn yelled, enjoying the thrill as the colorful silks sped by. Triton was in second place on the outside, but Time to Fly maintained the advantage on the rail by a half-length as they moved into the turn. The horses flew up the backstretch, with Triton gaining on the lead runner. He pulled into first at the top of the stretch with Time to Fly holding his own and Normandy Star half a length behind. Caitlyn gripped the rail and held her breath, feeling the thundering hoof beats vibrate in her chest.

The announcer shouted his report. "And Triton takes the lead!" Caitlyn and Danny's horse surged forward, all heart and strength. He was a beautiful sight as he stretched into his full stride.

But then, Triton faltered. In a split second, the majestic horse gave up his hard-earned gain. In two more seconds, he dropped back, losing any hope of the win—or even placing. The fourth-place runner seemed to lag with him as Time to Fly lunged forward and sailed across the finish line. Caitlyn watched the racers through her small binoculars. It seemed as though Guillon's jockey sat back in the saddle in the last second of the race, shifting his weight to slow his horse. Normandy Star came in second, with a black colt named Veloce landing third.

"Congratulations, Guillon!" Caitlyn squeezed his arm and tried to sound pleased for his second place standing.

He caught her up in his arms and spun her around. "I won!"

Confused, she said, "But Normandy Star came in second."

"Yes, but I won a major bet. I just won the trifecta!"

"What?" Caitlyn scrunched her brows in confusion.

"I placed a small fortune on Time to Fly, Normandy Star, and Veloce to come in first, second, and third!"

"You're kidding! That's incredible, Guillon!" She smiled but couldn't help thinking it was a little *too* incredible. Had his jockey purposefully slowed Normandy, so he'd come in second? "I'm so happy for you," she lied. "But I'm worried about what happened to Triton. I was sure he was going to win when he took the lead. Or at least finish in the top three, but then he dropped all the way back into the pack."

"You never can tell what will happen in the final stretch." Guillon beamed with pleasure. His gaze searched the people in the crowded stands, and Caitlyn noticed him offer a casual salute to someone below. She followed his line of sight down and saw him. *Trova!* The man they'd been searching for was in the crowd and responded to Guillon's gesture with a wide grin.

Others in the box surrounded Guillon to clap his back and congratulate him, and Caitlyn took the opportunity to text Dirk: **Trova is here! East side grandstands, row 4 or 5. Get him!**

"Come." Guillon murmured in her ear. His hot breath sent a warning shudder down her spine. How long had he been standing behind her? Had he read her text to Dirk? Guillon gripped her hips and directed her to the back of the viewing box. His presence behind her—his sneaking up without her awareness—sent her nerves into a panic. Vague images of her abduction last summer flew through her mind like evil specters. Caitlyn's head swam, weakening her knees. Her heart accelerated, forcing her breath to keep pace as Guillon pushed her into the shadows.

24

Colt's thigh jerked as though someone had struck him with a searing, red-hot iron rod. His leg burned. Silence followed the sharp echoes of the shots fired in the canyon. He ran a hand across the pain point and his fingers came up bloody. Burroughs's bullet had hit him. Surely, it wasn't anything that needed more than a stitch or two. He rolled to his hands and knees, pushed himself to his feet, and limped as fast as he could to his Jeep.

After wrapping his thigh tight with his scarf, he chased Burroughs down the canyon with flashing lights and a blaring siren. He called for backup, hoping Wes could make it to the mouth of the canyon in time to block Burroughs from driving into town. Colt kept his speed manageable, but fast enough to maintain a visual on the hatchback. Burroughs was sliding and skidding all over the road in his two-wheel drive. With the dusk deepening and the temperature dropping, Burroughs would be lucky to survive the twists and turns of the road. The waters of Moose Creek ran fifty feet below off the right side of the highway, and Burroughs wouldn't be the first driver to go over the edge if he didn't slow down.

One more mile before the canyon road flattened and entered the town. Wes's squad car was not there yet, and the hatchback raced on, flying through a four-way stop sign. Sparks flew as his undercarriage scraped the train tracks and he sped into the heart of town. Burroughs's tires slid when he skidded into a left turn onto Main Street. Colt slowed down, not wanting to cause an accident with innocent people in town.

"Cooper, what's your 10-20?"

"Just turning onto the Mountain Highway."

"We're already out of the canyon. I'm on Burroughs's tail, headed north. Square off and intercept him at Main and 8th."

"Roger."

Colt ignored the pain shooting up his leg into his hip. He gritted his teeth and turned onto Leopold Street, which paralleled Main, and clicked off his siren. With any luck, Burroughs might slow down if he believed he lost Colt in the chase. Unfortunately, the scream of twisting and crunching metal accompanied by the sound of breaking glass dashed his hope, and Colt swallowed hard. He cranked the steering wheel to the right at the next street and raced toward Main.

Burroughs had blown another stop sign, and an oncoming Chevy truck smashed into the side of his car. Colt jumped from his Jeep, but his injured leg buckled under him, and he fell to his knee. He sucked in a frozen breath and got back to his feet. By the time he made it to the accident, the driver of the truck was helping his wife and two kids out of the cab. Burroughs's empty wreck steamed in the cold, but Burroughs was nowhere to be seen.

Colt panned the gathering crowd. "Everyone, get inside!" he yelled. "Get inside and stay down."

A boy Jace's age, carrying a sled, pointed to the quilt shop across the street. "I saw him go in there, Sheriff."

Colt bit down on a sudden fear. Jace had said he was going to go sledding today, too. Was his son somewhere in the nearby crowd? He could be in real danger. The power of a parent's primal fear rocked Colt, but he shook his head hard, clearing his mind to focus on the situation at hand. He reached for the radio on his gun belt and called Wes.

"Coop, Burroughs hit a truck on Main. He is now in or near the quilt shop. Check the alley behind the stores on that side. I'm going in."

A little bell tinkled when Colt opened the glass paneled door. The store was warm. Its cheerfulness clashed with the danger lurking inside. Minnie Prue, the shop owner, cowered behind the cutting table. Colt held his index finger to his lips motioning for her to be quiet and he bent low, taking cover behind the rows of bolted fabric. He searched aisle by aisle through the bright prints.

A gun fired, and a quilt hanging on the wall above Colt's head exploded into white fluff and shredded calico. "Give it up, Burroughs," Colt yelled. "You're surrounded. There's no way out."

"Not a chance, Sheriff. I have nothing else to lose but my freedom." Burroughs dashed through the door to the back room.

Colt followed. Crouching low, he leaned against the wall to the side of the doorway. He peered around the corner, drawing two more shots. The door frame splintered, and the plaster board inches above his head crumbled. A flush of cold adrenaline filled his head and ran through his veins. Aiming his pistol around the corner, Colt scanned the space for innocents before he fired. He missed his target and Burroughs escaped through the back door into the alley. Colt pushed through the burning in his thigh to run after him.

More shots were fired outside before Colt threw the heavy back door open. A siren sounded, and Wes, who was in the alley to Colt's left, shielded himself behind the open door of his squad car. He yelled for Burroughs to stop, but Burroughs sprinted away in the opposite direction.

"Freeze, Burroughs!" Colt yelled. The man turned and raised his gun. Colt fired two rounds. Both hit Burroughs center mass. He fell, clutching his chest, onto the alley's icy gravel.

Burroughs's body lay still on the ground, curled into a fetal position. His eyes remained closed. Colt called out to check on Wes.

"I'm good, Sheriff."

Relieved, Colt held his gun pointed at the unmoving body. Step by cautious step, Colt hobbled toward the man he'd shot. He knocked Burroughs's gun away from his reach before kneeling down and checking his carotid artery for a pulse.

Burroughs was alive—barely. Colt yelled, "Wes, call an ambulance!"

Colt assessed Burroughs's gunshot wounds. The man had taken two 9mm rounds. One to the right side of his sternum, the other in his upper gut. He'd lost a lot of blood, already. Removing his own coat, Colt wadded it up and pressed it against the man's wounds. He checked Burroughs's pulse again, but it had stopped. Immediately, Colt began chest compressions.

"Come on, Burroughs, you son-of-a-bitch. You aren't getting off this easy. You have too much to answer for." Ignoring his own pain and the ringing that vibrated in his ears, Colt worked to keep Burroughs alive until the ambulance arrived.

As soon as the paramedics got there, Colt turned the lifesaving work over to them. Wes helped them lift Burroughs onto a stretcher and into the van. The driver rushed to transport Burroughs to the ER while Colt stood impatiently waiting for the other EMT to check his wounds as well. After the medic cleaned, sutured, and bandaged the gunshot wound on Colt's leg, he tended to his smaller cuts and scrapes. "I've patched you up, but you'll still need to have Doc Kennedy check you out."

"Yeah, okay," Colt said. "But first, we have to check on the family that was in the accident on Main." Colt and Wes, along with the paramedic, made their way back to the street. Colt interviewed the driver while his deputy questioned the other witnesses, and the paramedic confirmed no one else was hurt.

"Wes, you're on the accident report. When you're finished, call for a tow truck to haul Burroughs's car to the impound lot. I'm going to the hospital to keep an eye on his condition." The stitches in Colt's thigh pulled and burned as he got into his Jeep and drove across town.

25

Dirk's phone vibrated, and he read Caitlyn's text. He glanced up at Favre's private box and followed the man's gloating gaze down to the man Dirk had been chasing for well over a year. Anthony Trova! He was there, less than a hundred feet away. A hum of anticipation zinged through Dirk's chest. This capture had been such a long time coming.

Excusing himself, Dirk pushed through the crowd toward his quarry. Moving through the mass of bodies was like swimming upstream, and he accidentally bumped into an elderly woman. "Pardon me, ma'am."

"Watch it!" The woman screeched. "Who do you think you are?"

Her high-pitched tone caused people to turn and stare. One of those people was Anthony Trova. A spark of recognition lit Trova's soulless eyes as Dirk shoved his way through the crowd toward him. Trova turned to run, but a similar wall of humanity held him in place. Ten more feet and Dirk would have him. Finally.

Trova reached into the breast pocket of his suit coat and drew out a gun. A woman next to him screamed, and he grabbed her by the arm, pulling her in front of his chest, he used her as a shield. Her eyes bulged and her mouth gaped as she stared up at Trova, first with confusion, then in utter terror.

"Stay back!" Trova held the gun to her temple and yelled over the screaming throng. "Everyone, get back!"

The mob of people shoved and scrambled, running toward the exits. They pushed smaller folks to the floor, trampling them down. A gap formed between Trova and him. Dirk pulled out his gun as well, and he leveled it at the man's head. "Drop your weapon, Trova. There is no way out of this. No reason to make it worse on yourself." He glanced up at Favre's box for Caitlyn, but she was no longer there.

"You're wrong, Deputy. I'm going to walk right out of these stands with my new friend here, and you're going to let me, or I will splatter her brains all over the seats."

"You shoot her, and I'll shoot you. What do you gain?"

Trova dragged the woman back several steps scraping her heels on the concrete. One of her shoes came off. "I think I can shoot her and still have time to kill you. Your gray matter can mix together with hers along with the rubbish on the floor."

"That's not going to happen. There is no way you're walking out of here a free man. Drop your weapon. Do. It. Now!"

Trova yanked the woman tighter against his chest, knocking her hat to the side of her head. He held her by a fistful of hair and his arm around her neck. Tears smeared black streaks of mascara across her face and red lipstick smudged her cheek. She looked like a frightened Picasso painting. "You're the one who's going to drop his weapon." Trova pointed his pistol straight up in the air and fired. The woman screamed, and her knees buckled. Trova jerked her to her feet by her throat. She clutched at his hand trying to breathe while pieces of splintered grandstand roof fluttered to the ground around their feet.

"Okay, okay." Dirk was surrounded by screaming and panicked faces. There were too many people to risk any kind of gunfight, and he wanted to save the woman in Trova's grasp. Where was Reed? He needed her backup. She had to have heard the gunshot. Dirk held up his hands. He let his weapon swing from his forefinger hooked inside the trigger housing. "I'm putting it down."

He kept his left hand in the air with his palm open, as though in surrender. When he bent down to set his gun on the cement, he scanned the crowd, assessing his options. Without Caitlyn and Renegade on his side, there weren't many. Dirk rested his weapon on the floor at his feet.

Trova laughed and leveled his gun at Dirk's head. "You're a fool."

From somewhere above, a furry arrow streamed through the air and rammed into Trova's body, knocking him and his hostage to the ground. Vicious sharp teeth flashed in the midday sun before they sunk deep into the muscles and bone of Trova's gun arm. The mafioso screamed out in agony and released the woman in his grip. He flailed at the jaws clamping down on him, attempting to fight off the phantom K9 attacker.

"Renegade!" Dirk snatched up his pistol and lunged toward Trova. "Good dog!" Renegade flung his head from side to side causing Trova to screech. The dog's powerful fangs shredded the fugitive's flesh. Finally, Trova stopped fighting him and Renegade held the man down while Dirk frisked him for secondary weapons. He found a knife in Trova's sock, and a second gun holstered at the small of his back. Dirk handcuffed the man he'd been hunting for over a year. The action filled him with a sense of elation and relief. When he was fully in control of the situation, he shot his gaze up to the private box, but Reed was still nowhere to be seen.

REMEMBERING the tools she'd learned from her therapist, Caitlyn purposely slowed her breath and focused on counting to five as she breathed in, holding for five, and breathing out for the same count. She repeated the exercise as she reminded herself that she was competent. Not only competent, but *excellent* at physically defending herself, and she could handle Guillon Favre.

"Where are we going?" Caitlyn willed her body to relax, pretending to comply though instinctively she wanted to resist him. She wished Renegade was his normal self. He'd have been welcome company wherever Guillon was taking her, but the last time she saw him, he was still sleeping off the Xylazine.

Guillon pushed her through the private restroom door at the back of the box. Once inside the small room, he locked the door behind him.

"What are you doing?" Alarms blared inside her skull as Caitlyn turned to face him, positioning her feet to give herself a firm foundation from which to fight.

Guillon brushed his hands back over her cheeks and held her head between his palms. "I want to celebrate this moment with you in private." He crushed her mouth with an intense and forceful kiss. His teeth cut across her lips, drawing blood. She tasted the metallic tang.

Caitlyn pushed against his chest. "Guillon, stop. You're hurting me."

He responded by grabbing her wrists and forcing her hands above her head. He slammed her against the wall, leaning against her and trapping her with his body. Images of Elgin Payne blazed across her mind. Hot needles of panic shot into her scalp and through her body. Her knees wavered. The same terror she'd experienced when that monster held her captive last summer threatened to paralyze her now. It all rushed back, and she saw Payne's face superimposed on Guillon's. She felt the heat of Payne's blood on her hands and the weight of his body when he collapsed on her in his final moments of life after she had plunged her knife into him. Caitlyn fought for breath and an escape from the debilitating memories.

"Get off of me!" she gasped. She pushed against him, trying to squirm away. But Favre crammed her body firmly against the wall and yanked up the hem of her dress, tearing the fabric of her skirt. Caitlyn took command of her mind and forced her lungs to draw in air. She held her breath and prepared herself for defense.

As the seam of her dress ripped up her leg, her knee followed. She smashed him as hard as she could in the crotch and immediately stomped down on his foot, grinding the sharp heel of her shoe into him. Guillon's eyes widened and watered as he groaned. He bent over, but instead of backing off, he threw a backhanded uppercut and punched her in the face. Caitlyn deflected the swing with her forearm, but not before it connected against her chin, slamming her head into the wall. Pain radiated through her skull, and she blindly gripped his wrist. His other hand clutched her throat, cutting off her air.

Caitlyn's mind cleared instantly. She had only seconds of consciousness before the lack of blood to her brain would shut her down. Releasing his punching hand, Caitlyn clawed at the fingers on her neck. She grabbed hold of his wrist. Pressing down, she effectively glued his hand to her chest. Swinging with her free arm, she connected with a sharp crack at the back of his elbow. She twisted him away and down. Ramming her knee up with every ounce of fight she had, she crashed it into his face, busting his nose. Blood erupted like a volcano as Guillon screamed in agony. With the momentum of his falling body, she wrenched his dislocated elbow behind him and followed him to the floor. She ground her knee into his kidney, pinning him down as she reached for the Glock strapped in her thigh holster.

Caitlyn yelled, "Keep both hands behind your back where I can see them, you disgusting pig! You are under arrest!"

Favre coughed blood. "All I wanted was to enjoy my victory with you. I can't believe you attacked me like this." Even now he plied his seductive lies.

"*I* attacked *you?*" She couldn't believe his gall.

"You kneed me in the balls. I had to defend myself." He closed his lids and grimaced with pain. "And what do you mean I'm under *arrest?*" His hate-filled eyes glared up at her again. "You're a cop?"

"I'm a Deputy US Marshal, you idiot. You picked the wrong woman to force yourself on today." She reached for her purse and pulled out a heavy-duty zip tie. Reholstering her weapon, she brought his uninjured arm together with the other and bound his wrists.

He cried out in pain but kept on with the gaslighting. "I thought we had something special. I thought you wanted me as much as I wanted you." A self-deprecating smile slid onto his face, and he looked up at her through thick dark lashes. "You've been giving me mixed messages all along. That's not my fault. You can't arrest me for responding to your advances. You've been coming on to me for three days. I was simply confused. This is entrapment."

"I imagine that line of crap has worked for you in the past, Favre, but not with me. When a woman screams 'get off of me,' she means it. Nothing unclear about that." She ran her hands over his torso and down his legs checking him for weapons, but he had none. "Besides, I'm arresting you for selling illegal guns and running drugs, too. Your being stupid enough to think you could force yourself on me is just a bonus. We have sufficient cause with those charges alone, but I'm sure there will be many more complaints filed against you in the next several hours."

"You can't possibly have any evidence to prove those

charges. My attorney will have me out of jail in less than fifteen minutes."

"Yeah, yeah. Don't count on it. Deputy Marshals found Rutledge in Puerto Rico, and he's had plenty to say." Once she had Favre fully subdued, she called Dirk's phone. She gestured with her chin. "Get up." Guillon took his time climbing to his feet, and Caitlyn pressed his chest to the wall.

"Where are you?" Dirk shouted through the receiver.

"I'm in the private restroom at the back of Guillon's VIP-box. I just arrested him. Tell me you got your man."

"*I* didn't... but Renegade did! You should have seen him! He flew from the balcony of the spectator box like Super-dog or somebody. You're gonna have to get him a cape. Trova was holding a woman at gunpoint, but your dog knocked him away from her and tore the hell out of his shooting arm. He held Trova on the floor until I cuffed him."

"That's my boy! Is he okay?"

"Yeah, he's currently being slathered with appreciation from the woman whose life he saved and her friends. I think the attention is going to his head. He's going to be hard to live with after this." Dirk chuckled. "The local cops have Trova and are taking him to jail at their precinct."

"I'll bring Favre down. Can you call for another cruiser?"

"You got it."

Caitlyn unlocked the bathroom door and shoved Favre out of the small room. The box was empty of people. The wealthy revelers had already left to attend race-oriented dinners and parties. She took hold of Favre's good arm and escorted him down the stairs to where Dirk stood watching from behind his dark glasses.

When Renegade saw Caitlyn, he bounded up the steps toward her, leaving his adoring fans behind. Once she was on the main walkway, Ren bounced around her like a jackrabbit.

Dirk pulled off his sunglasses, his eyes narrowing as he studied her. He touched her cheek with his fingertips. "You're gonna have quite a shiner."

"Nothing compared to the blackeyes Favre's broken nose is going to give him." She grinned and passed Guillon off to Dirk. Caitlyn knelt down and threw her arms around her dog. He slathered her face with slobbery K9 kisses. The tension of the day melted away with his antics and the return of his normal, high-energy self.

26

Caitlyn and Dirk waited for paramedics to tend to Favre before local police took him into custody. She winced when the EMT forcefully straightened the man's aquiline nose. She looked away from the scene and up at Dirk. "Ren and I are going to go check on Danny. Something happened to Triton during the race, and I want to know what it was. Favre won a huge amount of money with a trifecta bet after Triton fell back, and I don't believe for one second that was a coincidence."

"You think Favre rigged the race somehow?"

"I do, but I don't know how. Yet." Caitlyn tugged at the skirt of her dress. The ripped seam slit up to her hip. "Can I borrow your windbreaker?"

Dirk slid out of the thin USMS jacket with the large block letters on the back identifying him as a US Marshal and handed it to her.

She tied the arms around her waist, covering the torn fabric. "Thanks. I'll call you after I talk to Danny."

"You ought to put some ice on your face."

"I will. Later."

Caitlyn couldn't wait to get out of the nonfunctional high-heeled shoes she wore with her dress, though the pointy heel did give Favre a nice extra jab when she stomped his foot. The thought filled her with a smug sense of satisfaction.

She and Ren made their way down the stairs of the grandstand and over to the stables. When they got there, Danny and the groom were rubbing Triton down. She leaned against the stall opening. "What happened out there? I thought Triton was going to win, but then he lost ground."

Danny dropped the cloth he was using into a bucket and crossed his arms over his chest. "I'm not sure. He felt strong and was surging forward beautifully. He was clear of the other horses, and everything was smooth sailing, but then it seemed like the steam ran out of him. He just stopped striving. He even stumbled on his way back to the stables. I was worried, so I had the vet check him over. She took some blood and did a few other tests. Hopefully, we'll know something soon. I'll go see if she's found anything yet." He left the stall and headed toward the vet's office at the end of the stable row.

Caitlyn pulled off her shoes and slid into a spare pair of muck boots. She picked up a dandy brush and starting grooming Triton's coat where Danny left off. She'd made two passes when yelling at the far end of the breezeway drew her attention. Caitlyn peered out of the stall.

Danny stood in the middle of the aisle facing a man who was yelling at him. "I put five grand on you to place and you fell back to fifth! I lost everything. You're gonna pay me back the money you owe my boss *and* the money I lost on you today."

Caitlyn and Renegade ran to Danny's side. When she got there, she saw that the angry man was holding a gun pointed at Danny. He swung the muzzle toward her. "This is none of your business, Missy. Get out of here."

Caitlyn yelled, *"Drz!"* and dove at Danny, knocking him to the ground. Renegade obeyed her command and leapt at the man's gun hand, clamping his mighty jaws down on the gunman's wrist. He screamed in pain.

Caitlyn drew her own weapon and retrieved the gun the man had dropped in the dirt. She pointed her Glock at the writhing man and called Renegade off. "Danny, pull the noseband from the bridle hanging on the door." She pointed at a spare headstall. Danny jumped up and thrust the leather strap toward her. Caitlyn lashed the man's wrists together with the leather band and told Danny to call 911. She frisked her captive, and finding no other weapons, she left him on the ground. While they waited for the police, she asked, "What's going on here, Danny? Is this about today's race? Did you throw it?"

"No! I swear I didn't. Something happened with Triton, but it had nothing to do with me. I owe this guy money, that's all. I borrowed cash from him to feed my family and to keep us in our apartment for another month. That's all. My payment to him is past due. It's why I needed to win today. But thanks to Triton, I'm further in debt than I was before."

"How much do you owe?"

The bound man rolled to his side. "This little puke owes my boss fifty-grand."

Danny's face was wane, and Caitlyn wondered if he was going to be sick. "That's way more than you'd need for rent and groceries."

"The interest rate is 80% and compounds daily. There's no way I can catch up unless I bet big and win." Danny's voice rose an octave. "Today was my chance, but I lost it all."

"Did you arrange for the horse thieves to steal those horses from the Pegasus Farm? Was that part of your payment?"

Danny's eyes shot to the side, then he dropped his gaze to the ground. "It wasn't part of *my* payment, but I admit, I knew about it. Before he left town, Mr. Rutledge told me to put the two horses in the end stalls. That someone was going to come for them in the night and that I was to stay out of the way."

"Someone Rutledge owed money to?"

"Yeah. Somebody called The Banker. The horse that won—the one called Normandy Star—is actually one of the Pegasus horses that was stolen." Danny wouldn't meet Caitlyn's eye.

"Guillon Favre's horse? And you knew about it? We were here looking for the stolen horses, and all along you knew?"

"I needed you to convince the Marshals to let me race because I'm desperate for the money. That's why I'm here. I never told you that Normandy was one of Mr. Rutledge's horses because he told me to stay out of it. I figured it was an insurance thing or something."

"What about the other horse that was stolen?" The pieces of the puzzle shifted, and Caitlyn saw them fit together.

"That's the funny thing. The thieves were supposed to take Triton too, but they went to the wrong stall and ended up with a different horse. I knew Triton could beat the horse they're calling Normandy. So, this was my chance to win big and get out of debt." Danny shrugged and stepped out of the way for the police officers who arrived to arrest the man lying face down in the dirt. "The other horse they stole was one Mr. Rutledge had for sale because he wasn't a promising racer."

"Danny! Caitlyn!" They both turned to see Dr. Pope hurrying toward them. "I'm glad I found you together. I did some tests on Triton's blood sample. I found evidence of Xylazine, the same tranquilizer I found in Renegade's blood. What I can't figure out is how Triton made it to the starting gate after being dosed. It's a fairly fast-acting drug."

The memory of light flashing off the gate assistant's hand in Triton's gate seconds prior to the race struck Caitlyn. "What if someone dosed him inside the starting gate?"

The vet crunched her brows together and then turned accusing eyes toward Danny.

He flung his arms out to his sides and red blotches formed on his cheeks. "I didn't do it!"

"I thought I saw something, but I was too far away. Could the guy on the gate crew have injected him?"

Dr. Pope released a long breath. "I suppose it *could* happen. Triton's adrenaline and amped up metabolism would burn through the tranquilizer fast. That might explain why it took half a minute for it to take effect. Did you see a syringe or anything like that, Danny?"

"No, I swear. I needed to win. Why would I drug Triton?"

Caitlyn recognized the logic in his answer. "It was Favre. He had to cause Triton to fall out of the race so he could win. And I'm convinced it was Favre who had Renegade drugged, too."

Dr. Pope tugged on the stethoscope looped around her neck. "I'll have all the horses in that race tested right away. We'll have a clear picture of what happened soon. If there were drugs involved, the race won't count." She turned on her heel and marched toward her office.

"Danny, you need to go to the police station. You're a part of this mess. If you're lucky, they'll probably go easy on you if you confess you knew about the horse theft and tell them everything else you know."

Caitlyn and Renegade left Danny with a local officer and took the truck to the police department in search of Dirk. She found him in an interrogation room with a Panama City detective and Guillon Favre. She flung open the door.

"Favre, you had my dog drugged." Behind her, Renegade's growl rumbled low and threatening as Caitlyn glared at Guillon.

He did his best to return her glower with a look of insolence, but the effect was comical with his black eyes and nose splint. "It's your own fault, Caitlyn—if that's your real name. You showed up with Pegasus's Triton and your ridiculous dog. Triton belongs to me. I paid Rutledge for him."

"You paid Rutledge for the privilege of stealing him, you mean."

"I paid him for the horses. He instructed me to have them picked up in the middle of the night. It's not my doing that Rutledge claimed they were stolen and what he does with his insurance company has nothing to do with me."

"It doesn't work that way," Caitlyn scoffed and pulled out a chair. She perched on the edge and leaned over the table toward Guillon. "So, when Triton ran so well in his first race, you decided to slow him down. That's it, isn't it? With him out of the running, you had the outcome in hand."

Favre's shoulders slumped. "I knew something was off about you from the very beginning. I wondered if you were following me for your uncle... when I believed Rutledge was your uncle. When you showed up at the race looking so..." His gaze slid over her suggestively making her shudder. "Your dog needed to be neutralized. For my own safety, of course," he smirked. "My driver took care of the details."

Caitlyn's fingers itched to slap the smug look off his face. "Yeah? How'd that work out for you?"

Favre tossed his chin at her. "Obviously, my man didn't give Renegade enough of the sedative. He should have put him to sleep for good."

Rage boiled in Caitlyn's blood, and without thinking she lunged at him. Renegade released a round of angry barking as she grabbed Favre by the collar of his shirt. "You're going to rot in prison!"

Sterling clutched her shoulders. "Let him go, Reed. He's not worth your badge. After the FBI finishes building their case against him, he'll be going so far down the hole he won't be seeing the light of day for a very long time."

She released him with a shove and then jerked away from Dirk. "Come on, Ren."

Behind them on their way out, Favre chuckled as the door closed. "Not if I trade my testimony for witness protection."

27

Colt parked his Jeep in the special spot designated for his vehicle near the entrance of the hospital, and careful not to slip on the icy pavement, he limped in through the double doors. The reception nurse pointed him toward the ER and Burroughs's curtained-off bed. Colt slid back the yellow drape. Blake was standing next to the bed along with two ER nurses. All three took a step back, and Blake called out the time of death.

Though Burroughs was a criminal, a drug pusher, a murderer, and a general dirt-bag, Colt found no joy in the fact that he'd shot and killed a man. It was a terrible thing, to take a life. Any life. His head swam, and he grabbed the curtain to keep from falling.

Blake noticed Colt tipple and reached out to help steady him before the drape pulled out of the track on the ceiling. "Colt, why don't you sit down for a minute?" The doctor motioned to one of the nurses. "Will you please get the sheriff some water?" He turned back. "I think you're in shock." He helped Colt settle onto a nearby chair and pointed to the bandage on his leg. "What happened here?"

"I'm fine. A bullet nicked me, but it's all stitched up." Colt rubbed the back of his neck. "It's been a hell of a day."

"Sounds like it." Blake reached for the cup of water the nurse brought. "Thank you, and will you also bring him some orange juice and a warm blanket?" He smiled, and when his dimples popped the woman practically swooned.

"Of course, Doctor," she blushed. Colt closed his eyes rather than roll them.

Blake handed him the water. "I'd like to look at that wound." He washed his hands and slid on a fresh pair of latex gloves. Gently, he removed the dressing and inspected the wound and sutures. "Looks like the paramedic did a good job. Did he give you an antibiotic?" Colt shook his head. The nurse wrapped a heated blanket around his shoulders and Colt's muscles eased into it.

Blake reached for his prescription pad. "Is Caitlyn at home? Do you want me to call her?"

"No, she's still in Tennessee. I'll call her later."

"Do you need a ride home?"

Colt held up his car keys. "I'll be fine in a few minutes. Thanks, though." He was suddenly exhausted and over-whelmed with a ravenous need to hear Caitlyn's voice. He wished she was at the cabin waiting for him. Wished he could lose himself in her arms, bury his face in her hair.

After drinking the water and juice, Colt felt he was stable enough to drive, so he left the hospital. On his drive out to their cabin, he called Caitlyn. "Hey, babe."

"What's wrong?" Caitlyn responded to what he assumed was the tiredness in his voice.

"I've had a long day. We found out what's been killing the cattle."

"That's good. Is it contagious?"

"No. Dr. Moore studied lab results from all the dead animals and discovered both acetone and lithium in their blood." He started at the beginning of the story since he was reluctant to tell her he'd caught a bullet in his leg. He didn't want to worry her.

"Both those chemicals are used in the production of methamphetamine."

"Exactly. We put two and two together and realized the ranches that had lost cattle were all located along the creek. Dr. Moore tested the water and found the same toxins there."

"Oh, no."

"Yeah, so Dylan and I rode up the creek to see if we could find where the toxins came from and how they got into the water. We found a shack someone had built on BLM property and was using as a meth lab."

"That's incredible."

"Yeah, a HAZMAT team is there now, cleaning up the mess, but that's not the craziest part. On my way home from Reed Ranch, I pulled over a guy for driving too fast on icy roads with a broken taillight. You'll never guess who the driver was."

"Who?"

Colt told Caitlyn the story of pulling Burroughs over, the car chase, and the shoot-out. "I ended up shooting him."

Caitlyn was quiet for a while before she asked, "Is he dead?"

"Yeah." Colt blinked hard and swallowed, gripping the steering wheel so hard his knuckles whitened.

"Are you okay?"

"I will be."

"I'm sorry I'm not there with you."

"Me too."

Caitlyn asked, "You think the meth lab belonged to Burroughs?"

"Most likely. I'm betting the investigation team will find his prints all over up there."

"Well, the world will be a better place without him."

"Yeah." Colt wished that thought was more comforting than it was.

"I've had quite a day myself." Caitlyn went on to tell Colt about how Renegade had helped Dirk catch Anthony Trova and how the mob boss was connected to Guillon Favre. She filled him in on the horse theft and how Favre had both Triton and Renegade drugged. "It ends up that a team of Marshals hunted Charles Rutledge down at the Hipódromo Camarero Racetrack in Puerto Rico. He agreed to roll over on Favre if he and his wife could get into WITSEC. Trova was just a lucky bonus."

"Is Ren going to be okay?"

"Yeah, he slept off the tranq and is back to his usual animated self."

"Why did Favre have Renegade drugged? Did he suspect you were law enforcement?"

"Who knows?" Her sing-songy tone made Colt suspect she wasn't telling him the full story. But what could he say? He wanted to know why there was a picture in the news of her kissing Guillon Favre, but Colt hadn't told her his full story either. Some things were better off shared in person. Caitlyn changed the subject. "Danny was released from the Panama City PD, and he and I should be back at Pegasus Farm in a couple of hours. I'm looking forward to a long hot shower and my bed."

"I didn't realize you were driving. It must be the middle of the night there." He glanced at the clock on his dashboard. "I hate that your job takes you so far away. How soon can you come home?"

"I'll have to finalize a few things at the farm. I can't leave until the horses are all auctioned off."

Colt turned onto to the road that led to their cabin. "That sucks."

"I'm sorry. I know what you're going through, and I wish I was there to help you through it. It should only be a couple more days, though."

He parked the Jeep in front of the cabin, closed his eyes, and rested his head back against the seat. "Okay. I guess I'll just talk to you tomorrow." He barely heard her response as a wave of bleakness overcame his heart and mind, and he dropped his phone on the seat. He buried his face in his arms crossed on the steering wheel and let hot tears seep from his eyes.

28

Caitlyn dozed until noon the next day and might have slept longer if Renegade would have left her alone. Instead, he rested his chin on the mattress next to her ear and groaned. He licked her nose. She wiped her face with her arm and turned away. "Yuck, Renegade!"

He responded with a desperate sounding yip.

"Okay, okay. I'm getting up." Caitlyn rolled out of bed and aimed her still exhausted body toward the door. "You need to go out, and I'm desperate for a cup of coffee." She trudged down the stairs to the kitchen.

"Good morning." One of the deputy marshals assigned to run the property auction greeted Caitlyn from her makeshift desk at the kitchen table.

"Morning." Caitlyn slid open the glass door to let Renegade out before pulling a mug from the cupboard.

The deputy closed her laptop and leaned back in her chair. "You'll be happy to know we set the horse auction for tomorrow."

Caitlyn filled her cup with stale coffee left over from earlier and heated it in the microwave. She propped herself against the counter to wait for it. "That was fast. I'm glad Danny and I got back in time. Are the horses ready?"

"What do you mean?"

"Are they clean and brushed?"

"They've been fed, but I doubt they've had any more attention than that."

Caitlyn sighed and retrieved her hot drink. "They'll bring a better price if they're groomed nicely." She blew the steam off her coffee.

"Does it matter?"

"It should. The more money we get for them, the better it is for the taxpayers. They're the true victims in all of this. It's the honest citizens who get the shaft when jerks like Rutledge don't pay their taxes."

The woman shrugged and got up to stretch. "Well, you have the rest of the day to make them pretty."

Renegade returned to the door and waited for Caitlyn to let him in. She filled his food bowl and refreshed his water. "I'll call Danny and see if he wants another day's salary. If the other groom is still here, we can at least get the most valuable horses looking their best."

Caitlyn left Ren to finish his breakfast and ran upstairs to dress. She called Dirk. "What's the scoop with Favre? They won't let him into WITSEC, will they?"

"No need. He offered to roll on Trova, but we already have more than enough evidence of our own to convict him. No, Favre is going to face the music. You'll probably have to fly back to Florida to testify at his trial."

"Good. That dirtbag deserves everything that's coming to him. A pretty boy like him should make lots of friends in prison." She was still mad that he'd attacked her, but his most unforgiveable offense was harming her dog.

By dinnertime, Caitlyn and the two other barn workers had the stalls clean, and the horses brushed out. She spent extra time on the steeds that were sure to bring the highest dollar. Especially Triton, who'd proved his worth on the track. She slid her hand down his sleek neck. "I'm gonna miss you, boy. You're destined for greatness. I sure hope you go to the perfect trainer."

"Caitlyn?" Danny leaned against Triton's stall door. Renegade went to him and nuzzled his hand, and Danny patted his head.

"Hey, Danny. Are you finished?"

"Yeah. The horses are all looking pretty good, considering the short amount of time we had."

"I appreciate your help."

"I'm grateful for the extra day's pay." He kicked at the shavings on the stall floor. "I heard an early bid came in. Someone wants the whole farm. As is."

"Seriously? Who?"

"According to the marshal up at the house, it was an anonymous bid through some bank in New York City."

Something about that didn't sit well with Caitlyn, but she couldn't say why. Trova was from New York, but he was in custody. Besides, what would he want with a horse farm in Tennessee? She would have liked to meet the people who were buying the horses, to see their faces and watch how they were with the animals. But she had no real ownership here, and on the bright side, if one person bought everything, lock, stock, and barrel, she could go home. "Hopefully, the bid checks out."

"Yeah, fingers crossed. And I'm hoping whoever it is needs a barn manager and a jockey." Danny grinned.

Caitlyn clapped him on the shoulder. "I'll be sure you get a glowing recommendation."

"Thanks."

Caitlyn handed Danny the brush she'd been using. "Come on, Ren. Let's go find out when we can head for home."

DIRK ESCORTED Trova back to New York, where the mob boss would face the first of his many criminal trials. Dirk was happy to leave Guillon Favre in custody of the FBI and ATF. They could... and would... take credit for his arrest. They were welcome to the task of sorting out the details of Favre's violations with the marshals in Tennessee. The local Panama City cops were handling the racetrack fraud. Even Florida's Department of Fish and Wildlife was getting in on the action. They were the division who investigated crimes against animals, and therefore the illegal drugging of horses.

Trova sat next to Dirk in the back row of economy seats on the United 777 jet flying to Newark, with his cuffed hands covered by a sweater. His sport coat mostly disguised his bandaged arm and shoulder. Dirk adjusted his seat, trying to find some room for his knees in the cramped space. He canted his head toward his captive. "Whatever happened to your travel buddy?"

"What are you talking about?"

"Eddy Fesco, your RV road trip companion."

Trova's eyes sparkled, but his expression remained passive. "I don't know any Eddy Fesco."

"Don't bullshit me, Trova. You drove with him down to Savannah where you parked your RV at a campground and then flew to Panama City. Only Eddy wasn't in Florida with you, so where is he?"

Trova smirked and shrugged, then winced at the obvious pain the movement caused in the shoulder Renegade tore up. Dirk had called the Chief Deputy Marshal in Savannah before they boarded their plane. The chief reported the RV was no longer at the campground, and that the camp host said he woke two mornings ago to an envelope with a cash payment taped to the lot post. The RV was gone.

Fesco was a petty criminal compared to Trova, but their friendship was cause for concern. It was likely that Fesco would step in for Trova on the outside, while the mob boss continued to run his empire from his prison cell. Chasing organized criminals was like trying to wrangle the snakes on Medusa's head. When you caught hold of one, another viper appeared, ready to strike.

Dirk couldn't wait to dump Trova in the lap of the New York FBI office and NYPD and go home. He planned to take a long weekend and drive up to his hunting cabin in the mountains west of Butte. He'd probably have to snowmobile to get into the backcountry, but then he would catch up on some reading and enjoy the solitude. Someday, he hoped to share his remote getaway with someone special, but he had yet to meet a woman he trusted for more than a night or two. His chest ached again with loneliness, but old scars ran deep.

The jet landed and Dirk waited with his prisoner until everyone in the entire plane exited before he allowed Trova to get to his feet. A team of three FBI agents met them at the gate and drove them to Manhattan and the NYPD OCD building. It had been only days since Dirk was last here, but it seemed like months. He left Trova with an interrogation team and went to find Hank.

They were booked on a 7:15 flight to Billings out of La Guardia. This time, Dirk and Hank enjoyed the economy plus section with enough room to move their legs without grinding their knees into the hard plastic back of the seats in front of them. Dirk pressed his headphones into his ears, but he turned the sound down and only pretended to watch the action movie playing across the screen. It was his way of keeping to himself. He had plenty of days, months, and years ahead of him with Hank as his new rookie partner. The kid seemed sharp, and it shouldn't be difficult to help him assimilate as a deputy marshal in Montana. But for now, Dirk needed to decompress. His thoughts shifted to memories of Sam. The only people he'd ever felt close to his entire life were his ex-wife, his late-partner, Sam Dillinger, and Caitlyn Reed. Hannah had almost destroyed him, and now Sam was gone. Like it or not, Dirk knew it was time to move on.

TIM SMITHERS, formally known as Bill Hayes, stared at himself in the mirror and experienced an odd sense of self-detachment. He stood in the undecorated bathroom of a decent, cookie-cutter, suburban home in Bismarck, North Dakota. Hot water ran from the faucet, steaming up the glass as he prepared to shave.

His WITSEC Marshals had dropped him off at his new home yesterday afternoon. They gave him a new driver's license and social security card printed with the name Timothy Smithers. Would he ever get used to being called Tim? The marshals went over all the rules and left him with enough cash and groceries to get through a couple of weeks until he found a job. His immediate homework was to memorize and internalize his false past.

He'd testified against his boss Charles Rutledge, and later learned that Rutledge had also agreed to turn state's evidence against Guillon Favre—The Banker. Rutledge was also now in WITSEC somewhere in the vast United States. Briefly he wondered if Tansey Rutledge entered witness protection with him. He couldn't imagine her living a bland, middle class, suburban life.

That they were in the system too, seemed like an extra layer of protection as far as Bill—Tim—was concerned. And though this was a fresh start for him in many ways, it was also a form of prison. He was stuck so far up north that his southern blood was half frozen all the time, and he was now required to show up at some boring job, day in and day out. But he was alive and safe, and that said something. He still had nightmares of his drug deal gone bad, and this was the best option he was going to get. He was set up to live his best life... such as it was.

Tim dragged the plastic disposable razor down his cheek. Time to scrape off the old and step into the new.

29

On Saturday, Colt woke with the sun, but he lay in bed staring at the ceiling. His chest ached. The silence in the cabin had a lonely quality without Caitlyn and Renegade there. Hopefully, they'd be home by Monday. He had the weekend off and had promised to help Allison and Jace move into his house in town that morning. It would give him something to do and hanging out with Jace would brighten his mood.

He dragged himself to his feet and plodded barefoot across the cold floor to the kitchen to make a much-needed pot of coffee. When he walked, the sharp tug of the itchy stitches on his leg threw his thoughts back to the tragic events of the previous week. He clung to his gratitude that Burroughs's tirade through town had hurt no one else. Colt gulped several burning swallows of the strong brew, hoping to wash away his dark mood before he texted Dylan. His brother-in-law had offered to help with the move.

The men met on the street outside of Allison's parents'

house. Jace ran out the front door, excited to see them and play with Dylan's dog, Larry. "Hey, bud." Colt laughed and hugged his son when the boy crashed into him. "You ready to move your stuff to your new house?"

"I'm ready to have my own room. That's for sure." Jace smiled up at Colt before he threw a stick for Larry to chase. The dog bounded through the snow to hunt for it.

There wasn't much to pack up, just clothes and a few small pieces of furniture Allison's mom donated to them. They were able to load everything between the truck, Allison's car, and Colt's Jeep.

Colt slammed Dylan's tailgate closed. "That didn't take long. I guess it's a good thing I'm renting the house to you furnished."

Allison peered up at him. "Your things will be nice to have until I send for my own furnishings. I had the movers put all my belongings in storage when we moved out of our rental house in Missouri, but now I'll have to ship it here."

Colt bobbed his head. The finality of giving up his childhood home hit him with a wave of melancholy. "Just let me know. I'll move my furniture out whenever you're ready."

Jace and Larry raced over to them from the yard. "Yeah, and I'll finally get my bike back!"

Colt mussed his son's hair. "It'll be nice to have some wheels. Let's get you two moved in. Who are you riding with, Jace?"

"Larry." Jace grinned. The boy had already learned to navigate the tension between his parents.

"Alright, you guys go with Uncle Dylan. I'll see you

over there." Colt and Allison watched him gallop to the truck with Larry at his side.

"Dylan isn't really his uncle. I don't know why you insist on calling him that," Allison murmured.

"He's the boy's step-uncle. But that's too hard to say. You should be glad Jace has a whole family here. The Reeds love him, and he'll be a happier kid for it."

"I guess." She left to get in her car, and Colt followed suit.

Less than two miles away, they parked in front of Colt's old house and reversed the packing process. Allison stood in the center of the living room directing traffic and ordering the men to move furniture here and there to her liking. Colt and Dylan built Jace's new twin bed, matching nightstand, and dresser. Colt had ordered a baseball bat lamp and baseball themed sheets with a coordinating bedspread. Allison made up the room as Colt went back outside to bring in the last load from his Jeep.

He leaned into the back end to reach for a box of clothes when he noticed the wrinkled-up newspaper that Allison showed him the other day with the picture of Caitlyn kissing Guillon Favre. He knew she was under-cover, but that fact didn't prevent the oily feeling he got in his belly when he looked at the image. A dog paw tapped his leg, and he tore his gaze away from the newspaper. "I'm coming, Larry."

But it wasn't Larry's bark that echoed into his car. The sound was much deeper and louder. *Renegade!* Colt let the box drop, and he spun around. Renegade was at his feet, wagging his tail and spinning circles. Colt patted him but looked past the dog for Caitlyn. She stood on the opposite side of the street, leaning against her USMS K9 Explorer, smiling at him. Her long dark hair was twisted into a messy braid that hung over her shoulder.

"I didn't think you were getting home until tomorrow." He pushed past the excited dog and strode to his wife. She met him halfway, and he pulled her into his arms. He nestled his face in her hair and breathed in the familiar coconut scent. "I'm so glad you're here." The tension and anxiety he'd been carrying around since the shooting drained away as he held her. Sudden tears formed along the lower lids of his eyes, and he squeezed them shut. He swallowed a sob that swelled in his throat and let an immense wave of emotion flow silently through him.

"When I talked to you on the phone, you sounded like you needed a hug, so we came home as fast as we could." Caitlyn giggled as she wrapped her arms around his neck. Renegade barked at their feet and was soon joined by Larry.

"I need a hell of a lot more than a hug, but this sure feels great for now." He drew back and searched her eyes. He traced the fading bruise on her cheek and rage boiled in his belly. "What happened here?"

"It's nothing. Hazard of my occupation, and it's almost gone." Caitlyn looked away from him and dropped her chin. "I have something to tell you, though."

"What's wrong?"

"Well, I told you about going undercover as Rutledge's niece, right?"

"Yeah…"

"But I didn't tell you that Guillon Favre came on to me.

I let him kiss me." She paused to look up at him then. Colt felt his jaw stiffen, but he did his best not to show any emotion. He wanted her to tell him what happened. "It bothered me, a lot. But it was necessary to get him to trust me."

"And…"

"And then he took it too far. He attacked me. That's where the bruises on my face came from."

A wave of fury rolled through him, and Colt's hands bunched into fists. "Are you okay? Did he… What happened?" He bit the words out through clenched teeth.

Caitlyn placed her hands on his chest. "No. I'm fine. I promise. He got in a lucky punch, but he took the worst of it. And now he's in jail for a very long time." She stroked his cheek and stared into his eyes. "I'm okay, but I'm sorry. I feel bad about the whole thing."

He did his best to let the rage flow away. Catie was home, safe and sound. He pressed his lips against her forehead and then kissed her bruised chin. "I missed you, you know."

"I missed you too. It was two long days of driving, but Ren and I pushed through. I'm exhausted, but glad to be home. So incredibly happy to be home with you."

CAITLYN GAZED up at her handsome husband. She touched his face, running her fingertips along his square jawline. Her work had distracted her, and she had Renegade to keep her company, but now as she stood encircled in Colt's arms, she knew she never wanted to leave again—if she could possibly get away with it. "How much longer will you be helping Allison and Jace move in?"

"We're just about done, but I have Jace the rest of the weekend." His blue-green eyes looked wistful.

She smiled and tapped his nose. "That's okay. We can make a big pot of soup and play games by the fire. And maybe later, we'll draw up plans for the room addition on the cabin."

Colt nuzzled her neck, sending delicious tremors down her spine. "That sounds nice."

"I was hoping to bring home a big payout from the track to finance the construction. And I would have too if Favre hadn't drugged Triton so he could win the trifecta." She was still mad about the race and deeply angry at Favre for attacking her and for his indifference about the harm he could have caused Triton and Renegade.

"If you think about it, we won our own trifecta by bringing down Burroughs, Favre, and ultimately Trova."

Caitlyn laughed. "I guess you're right. I never thought about it that way. Too bad our trifecta doesn't pay out like the one at the track." Her smile dimmed as a pesky and insistent thought crossed her mind.

"What's wrong?"

"We took down those three... but we never found Trova's RV, or the friend he drove down to Savannah with."

"So?"

"So, it wouldn't surprise me if Trova's crime syndicate continues to thrive, only under the leadership of Trova's buddy." She let out a heavy sigh.

"That sounds like an NYPD issue, Catie. Not yours."

"I suppose. But an anonymous bidder purchased Pegasus Farms and all the horses. The bid came from a bank in New York. The case still feels unresolved, to me."

"No. You accomplished what you went to Tennessee for and more. This isn't your case anymore." He pushed a loose strand of hair behind her ear. "Besides, I'm hoping you'll be home for a while now."

She shook her head to chase away thoughts of crime bosses and smiled up at Colt's earnest expression. She stood on her toes and kissed his cheek. "I will. It's time for Renegade's requalification tests. So, we have to spend the next couple of weeks training. I have at least until the exam, for sure."

"And McKenzie wants to breed Renegade with Athena. Sounds like now would be the perfect opportunity." He slid an arm around her waist and led her toward the house. "Have you seen what they've done with their kennel? Kenzie and Dylan have set up a nice business. It's impressive."

Jace and Larry burst through the front door. "Renegade!" the boy shouted. As he darted past them, he waved. "Hi Caitlyn!"

"Hi Jace." Laughter bubbled through her words. "Boys and dogs."

"Maybe we should have more of those." Colt squeezed her playfully.

"Which?" She raised a speculative brow at him. "Boys or dogs?"

"Both!" He kissed the top of her head as they watched Jace bound through the snowdrifts with Renegade and Larry in his wake.

THANK YOU FOR READING
TRIFECTA

I HOPE you enjoyed the thrill of riding along with Caitlyn and Renegade on another adventure this time into the exciting and sometimes dark world of horse racing.

If you enjoyed reading Trifecta ~ Book 6 in the Tin Star K9 Series, I would be most honored if you would please write a quick review.

Review TRIFECTA

NEXT:

THE FIGHT FOR JUSTICE, Integrity, and Service with the US Marshals Service continues with the exploits of Deputy Marshal Dirk Sterling in the

Dirk Sterling - US Marshal Thriller Trilogy.

Order **EXTRACTION**
Book 1 in the
US Marshal - Dirk Sterling - Trilogy
at
Jodi-Burnett.com
and get the series prequel novella
FORGED

for Free!

For more of my books (and some Free Books) or to join my reader group, visit my website at Jodi-Burnett.com.
Jodi-Burnett.com

Extraction

Deputy US Marshal, Dirk Sterling, struggles to trust his new boss, Chief Emory Grey. In the few weeks Dirk has known her, Grey has already lied to him and proven to be something more than she seems.

Grey orders Sterling to lead a Federal Task Force to hunt down an international smuggler suspected of crossing the northern US border with an invaluable ancient artifact.

US government officials believe the sale of this priceless relic will be used to fund worldwide terrorism with the goal of destroying the world's most powerful governments. Will Dirk and his group of specialists recover the stolen artifact before it becomes the lynch pin of global destruction?

ACKNOWLEDGMENTS

First, and always, I thank God for blessing me with a vivid imagination, work I love, and for the inspiration with which to do it.

I am enormously appreciative for my team. I am beyond grateful to Kae Krueger who is the first to see my words and check my stories. A huge thanks to my team of beta readers who help me see the forest for the trees. You all are integral to my writing process. Thank you, Chris, Emily, Sarah, Jenni, Brooke, Jerry, Sheila, Elle, Barb, and Kay.

When I was writing Trifecta, I was in Florida for a writer's conference and had the opportunity to stop in at Tampa Bay Downs Racetrack. It was a Sunday in the off season, so no races were going on, but the sheriff's deputy who was on duty patiently answered all my questions and allowed my husband and I to roam all over the track. When I wrote about Panama City Downs—my fictitious racetrack—I had Tampa's track in my mind's eye. I'm so grateful to the staff there.

Thank you to the members of my business mastermind; Corinne O'Flynn and Dominika Best. Without your encouragement, I'd still be in the weeds. You women inspire and encourage me, and I'm blessed to have you in my life.

I could not do any of this without the support and encouragement of my family. Writing is a solo venture. Thanks for pulling me out of my cave and loving me through the rough spots. I cherish the inside jokes, all the sports, and most especially the way we love each other. My cup overflows.

Most of all, I thank my husband Chris, who helps me flesh out my plots, and reads all the words. He listens to my crazy ideas, accompanies on my grand adventures, puts up with my frustrations, and loves me through it all. I rely on his strength and encouragement. I love you, Chris, with all my heart. Thank you for believing in me.

ABOUT THE AUTHOR

Jodi Burnett is a Colorado native and a mountain girl at heart. She loves writing Mystery and Suspense Thrillers from her small ranch southeast of Denver, where she lives with her husband and their two big dogs. There she dotes on her horses, complains about her cows, and writes to create a home for her mysterious imaginings. Burnett is a member of Novelists, Inc. and Sisters in Crime. Connect with the author at Jodi@Jodi-Burnett.com. Get some free books by Burnett on her website.

facebook.com/JodiBurnettAuthor

twitter.com/jodi_writes

instagram.com/jodiburnettauthor

ALSO BY JODI BURNETT

\-

<u>US Marshal Dirk Sterling Trilogy</u>

<u>FORGED (Free Prequel)</u>

<u>EXTRACTION</u>